# The

# *Shrew*

**Nicholas Gordon**

Published by

**MELROSE
BOOKS**

An Imprint of Melrose Press Limited
St Thomas Place, Ely
Cambridgeshire
CB7 4GG, UK
www.melrosebooks.com

**FIRST EDITION**

Cover designed by Catherine McIntyre

**ISBN  978-1-906561-26-0**

Printed and bound in Great Britain by:
CPI Antony Rowe, Chippenham, Wiltshire

**FSC**
**Mixed Sources**
Product group from well-managed
forests and other controlled sources
Cert no. SGS-COC-2953
www.fsc.org
© 1996 Forest Stewardship Council

In Memory of

'Thistle'

If there is a heaven let it be on the edge of a wood in winter….

"This know also, that in the last days perilous times will come"

2 Timothy 3:1

'The Shrew' tells of one countryman's struggle to protect his livelihood and the traditions that he grew up with against a rising tide of terror and destruction.

When Victor Drew the gamekeeper at the Brockleston shoot receives a threatening letter from what appears to be a group of animal rights activists he becomes concerned for the security of his job and the continuation of sporting activities on the estate. He knows that Richard Mowbray, Lord Hugo Brockleston's land agent, has no loyalty to the long-standing traditions of the estate. Mowbray would gladly replace the shoot with any more profitable enterprises to fund his absentee employer's extravagant lifestyle in the Bahamas, thus protecting his own post in the bargain. Victor cannot imagine the size of the storm that is just over the horizon or the strength of the forces stacked against him and the shoot.

*The work is purely fictional and any similarity to persons alive or dead is purely coincidental.*

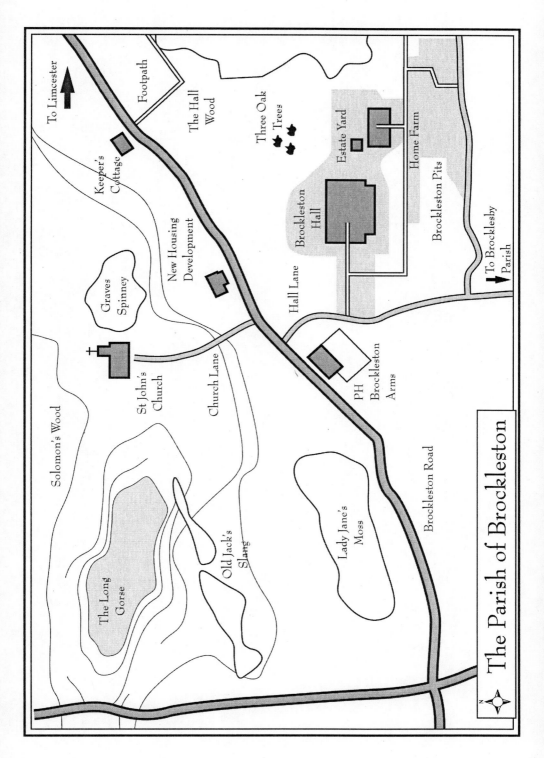

The Parish of Brockleston

# *Chapter One*

I<small>T WAS A DAY LIKE</small> any other working day in October; the nagging wind hinted at oncoming rain and the clouds rolled across the distant hills, as dark and depressing as Victor Drew's current mood. He trudged on through the peaty mud that lay thick in the ride which cut through Solomon's Wood, his black Labrador bouncing along beside him, as excited as always despite his lengthening years. He hardly noticed the dog at all, his constant companion of the last ten seasons obscured from his mind by his black mood. It was almost half past three and it was going dark early, the daylight fading prematurely as the storm clouds gathered. He had six other feed hoppers to fill before he could call it a day and they were spread across two of the largest woods on the shoot. Suddenly the distinctive 'rusty hinges' shriek of a cock pheasant echoed from within a nearby rhododendron; the Labrador darted into the bush after the bird. Victor was shaken from his thoughts and shouted at the dog, "Storm, you bloody mongrel, get back here now." The old dog sprang out of the tangle of leaves and branches and returned to his side, cowering in apology. Victor smiled to himself and patted the dog's head; he couldn't stay mad at his old friend, whose only crime was enthusiasm. By the time he had filled the last of the hoppers and checked the release pens in The Long Gorse, the rain had set in as predicted; he could already feel the chill of the water as it made its way through the holes in his worn out waxed jacket. His right shoulder ached as the damp aggravated an old injury. He made his way back to his old Land Rover across a field of maize stubble, the greasy wet clay clinging to his boots, making walking hard work as his feet slid backwards and sideways at each step. He suddenly got a strange feeling that someone was watching him; he looked up from the slimy clay and stubble and stared out across the fields to his left. He had not been mistaken; about 300 yards away, on the other side of a hedge, two figures in red waterproof

1

jackets were looking in his direction, their hoods up, keeping out the driving rain. He didn't really give them much thought. He just dismissed them as some townies in the latest colour of designer outdoor jackets taking in the quaint yokel and his dog. A story that would be later told during the coffee and mints at their next dinner party, he thought to himself with a wry smile. He opened the back door of the Discovery and old Storm jumped in without invitation, glad to be out of the weather. He took off his rain sodden coat and threw it in next to the dog. As he left the field gateway and entered the lane, turning left to drive towards the village and his home, his thoughts returned to the cause of the afternoon's bad mood. A letter, which had arrived in the post that morning, an unwelcome intruder into his life which now occupied his thoughts more than Saturday's opening shoot:

Dear Mr Murdering Gamekeeper,

If you think you're going to have another winter of fun with your toady employers, killing defenceless birds, think again.

We're onto you mate, so watch out, it's not going to be as easy this season. You and your bloated tweed clad cronies are going to pay.

How you can call what you lot get up to a sport is beyond us, give it up now before we make you!

The Animal Defenders.

At one time he would have dismissed it as the work of some socially inept crank, but in the current climate it looked far more sinister and as he was now the only keeper left on the shoot after the estate had 'downsized' its sporting enterprises, it worried him greatly. The current land agent of the Brockleston Estate was not a countryman and any bit of confrontation no matter how small might lead to him closing down the shoot altogether. The end of an era going back to Victor's grandfather's day and more pressingly the end of his job and occupancy of his tied cottage. Since the death of his father, Hugo, the current Lord Brockleston, had placed his total trust in Richard Mowbray his agent; any decisions Mowbray made regarding the estate were normally 'rubber stamped' without question. Hugo saw the estate as a business enterprise, its sole purpose to fund his lifestyle, which was centred on his luxury yacht and the social circle that he kept in the Bahamas. To Victor's knowledge, Hugo had only visited Brockleston on three occasions in the last five years, the last occasion being two years previous for his father's funeral and the business of transferring the estate. As Victor drove towards Brockleston village in the fading light and now torrential rain, his eyes caught what at first he thought was a leaf lying in the road just ahead of the Land Rover. The leaf moved and scurried in a circular motion; he realised it was a tiny shrew. It was too late to brake or swerve; Victor glanced in the rear view mirror a split second later; the shrew was still there in the centre of the lane, going about its business, known only to itself; an insignificant creature in the grand scale of things, but important to itself as we all are. He couldn't help pitying the creature, imagining it still being there when the next vehicle came down the lane; its life being ended by a rolling wheel, the driver being totally oblivious of its presence; the shrew's limited knowledge of the world being ended without prior knowledge or afterthought. The similarity to his own existence struck him like a cold piece of steel deep in his heart.

Victor arrived back at his cottage in the village. As he pulled into the short driveway past the collapsed wooden gates, which lay like two old battered dogs at the entrance, the rain seemed to come down even harder. The storm reached its zenith as the tyres crunched to a halt on the sodden chippings. Victor jumped out, ran to the back, grabbed the old Lab that was now lying comfortably on his coat and got himself and the dog in through the cottage door as quickly as he could manage. The whole process was so uncomfortable and hurried that it worked out just fine for the occupants of a small blue hatchback vehicle that just happened to be passing as he turned into his drive. The driver and passenger paid an unhealthy interest in the dilapidated dwelling as the vehicle slowly passed its entrance before speeding off out of the village in the general direction of the motorway and Limcester. There were no lights on in the house when Victor entered, nor was there a welcoming fire in the hearth or a smell of food coming from the oven of the ancient solid fuel cooker. Victor had lived alone for the last five years, apart from old Storm who rarely left his side. His late wife Susan had been taken from him at the whim of a 'boy racer' (as the hard-nosed traffic cop that dealt with the accident had described him). This happened one Saturday afternoon in a particularly hot June, as they were returning home from a trip to view some new pheasant poults in the next county. He threw a few small logs into the cooker to spark it up and get some heat going then turned to feeding old Storm. The Labrador was doing his usual manic dance around the kitchen at just the suggestion of food. Just as he was starting to consider food for himself, the telephone began to ring; he cursed and went to answer it. It was Mowbray; he cursed again under his breath.

"Ah Drew, how's things, everything ready for Saturday's show?" He hated these conversations with Mowbray at the best of times; they were never easy, but this time it was far worse, despite the fact he knew all was as it should be for that weekend's shoot. He had worked hard at all the little details his late father had taught him. The nagging fear and doubt that the letter had caused taunted him as he spoke to the agent. He knew he should really inform Mowbray about the threats, but doing so would play into his hands and strengthen his arguments against the continuation of sporting activities at Brockleston. So his silence regarding the matter was maintained as he assured Mowbray that all was ready and that good sport was guaranteed.

"Good man, see you at the shoot shed at 10am on Saturday then. I've a few matters to go over with you regarding the day's drives. Take care Drew." Mowbray rang off, the cottage was again silent, apart from the sound of an empty dog bowl scraping across the kitchen tiles as the old dog tried to extract the last microscopic fragments of his meal from inside it.

Victor prepared his own simple meal then sat silently in the old armchair next to the fire; he stared into the flames, his mind wandering, unable to relax. He had turned the television set on before he sat down; he did it out of habit but he rarely paid much attention to it, the room just seemed slightly less empty with it on. As he sat in the half-light of the room his thoughts turned to past times as they all too often did since the loss of Susan. The previous mention of the shoot shed triggered thoughts of an evening in June several years ago when she had still been with him. They had argued about something, it was hard to recall exactly what; no doubt some trivial matter or other that often causes tired couples to flare up with each other at the end of a hard day. He could remember being in a real rage almost to the point of hitting her. It hurt him to recall how angry he had been; it made the sense of her loss even sharper. He had walked out of the cottage, not thinking of where he was going or why; he just wanted to get away from her. He left so suddenly that not even Storm was able to follow. He walked a short distance up the lane out of the village and climbed over a stile onto an ancient footpath that crossed a pasture field; this had recently been cleared for silage. For once he was wearing what he would call `town` shoes and `going out` clothes, as they had intended to go out for the evening prior to the argument taking place. He had already got himself ready. He was not dressed for cross country travel. As he climbed over a fence and into an adjoining field he stepped down into long grass that had been left for hay. It was already damp with the condensation of approaching night and the moisture caused the fallen grass seeds to cling to his shoes and gather in the eyelets. He noticed this as he strode out across the field but paid little heed to it, such was his mood. In the corner of the hay field he came to a group of three old oak trees, huddled like old men in hiding from the 21st century, their little corner of the world having changed little in the few hundred years they had stood there through all weathers and wars. The grass under the trees was short, dead and dry; it had the pale creamy pink colour that low lying grass in these shaded and sheltered places always had at that time of year. Victor sat down with his back resting against the trunk of the central oak; it was like sitting with old friends, and they neither questioned nor judged, they were just simply there. The place was silent apart from the lonely ghostly calls of a pair of buzzards that circled high up above the three trees. He sat back and

5

watched the birds, feeling small, insignificant and sad, his anger gone, replaced with a feeling of emptiness and solitude. After a few minutes the sound of a tractor approaching from the far end of the field disturbed his thoughts; the field was being mown in preparation for the hay. Victor immediately took to the cover of the hedge, realising how ridiculous the sight of the gamekeeper sitting `dressed up` under an oak tree in the middle of nowhere would look. As depressed as he felt, he wasn't prepared to trade that for embarrassment. He slipped away through the hedge with the practised ease of a wild creature, even though he was dressed for a civilised night out. As he emerged on the other side another resident sat looking at him in total surprise and bemusement. Charlie fox had been on his haunches waiting for rabbits to leave the hedgerow; he fixed Victor's gaze for a few seconds before cantering off across the field. Despite his mood Victor smiled to himself at Reynard's surprise, feeling some respect and affection towards his constant bane around the pheasant pens. Victor walked on, now keeping in the lee of the hedgerows to hide his presence from others, as he always did when his thoughts were not clouded by the flames of bad temper. He found himself walking toward the Brockleston Home Farm, a collection of old farm buildings with the addition of a few modern livestock sheds which one of the tenants used to house pigs and cattle. The Home Farm had been one of the late Lord Brockleston's passions and he had taken great interest in the running of it in conjunction with his trusted farm bailiff Reg Jones. Now both men lay in the soil of Brockleston churchyard, no doubt spinning in their respective tombs at the thought of how untidy and uncared for the old place looked. The original farmyard was cobbled and it was surrounded by traditional red brick buildings which had slate roofs. To one side of the yard closest to the road lay what once had been a stable for the working horses. This was now what was referred to as the shoot shed and had been used as this ever since Victor could recall. Victor reached up to a little ledge by the door where the key was kept; he unlocked the door and went inside, no doubt the first person to enter since the last day of the previous season, the keeper's day on the first of February. The late evening light pierced through the dirty windows to one side of the shed. It shone across the trestle tables which were along three sides of the room where only mice had played for the last five months, no doubt eating what remained of discarded food crumbs left from countless midday and tea time gatherings of guns and beaters. Amongst the dust and mouse droppings a few tokens of last season still remained. An empty whisky glass, an old shoot card and a tweed cap lay on one of the tables, a beater's stick had been left by the two rows of nails where the bag of birds was always hung at the end of the day's shooting. Victor sat at the centre of the table that faced the windows, in the seat where the shoot captain always sat. Behind him on the whitewashed wall in scribbled pencil were dozens of dates and names, mainly records of who had won `the sweepstake` for the number of birds shot on a particular day. All written in a drunken relaxed hand at the end of another day spent with friends in the glory of the countryside. Some of the names would never be written again, there were some close friends that had shared a drink in the shed for a final time; his father being amongst them. He thought how strange it was to be in the place in such silence, almost like a surreal nightmare, a place that normally rang with good humour and friendship, sitting still and brooding like a forgotten tomb. He had never set foot in the place outside the shooting season before and had vowed never to do so again if unaccompanied; the thoughts were too strange to bear. He left the shed, locking the door and its strange feelings behind him, and made off across the fields towards home as darkness started to fall. There had followed a couple of days of only 'half' speaking to each other after the episode. But as usually happened they both got fed up with this and life then resumed as normal, rows between them were rare but when they did happen they were proper ones he thought as he smiled to himself, before getting up to stoke the fire and pour himself a whisky.

$$*****$$

About twenty-three miles and a whole culture away from Brockleston the small blue hatchback left the motorway and took the turning for the nearby town of Limcester. As it entered the town it headed for one of the rougher areas, the sprawling Brandley Park. A huge warren of a council estate, its reputation for being the local centre for drug dealing, handling stolen goods and any other criminal activity was well deserved. Since its construction back in the late 1960s it had quickly developed into a place where you only went if you lived there or had to visit under pressing circumstances. The hardworking decent folks who were forced to live amongst the criminal classes had their daily lives made a complete misery. Over the years, tens of thousands of taxpayers' pounds had been poured down the stinking drain of the area in the form of council schemes and police projects, all with little effect. It was a lost cause from the start. The two occupants of the car, an ageing Ford Fiesta, were no strangers to the members of the local constabulary. Apart from those areas of criminal activity that were deemed `unrespectable` by even the average career criminal, such as sex crimes, child pornography and the like, there were not too many avenues of crime that they had not travelled down over the years. The pair had met in a young offenders' institute when they were both serving time for vehicle related offences and burglaries early on in their careers; since then they had run together like a pair of wayward mink, leaving misery and despair as they went. Now in their late twenties, with plenty of hard earned experience regarding the methods of the police and criminal justice system behind them, they were not so easily caught out and relied far less on luck to keep them running free. The ringing of a mobile phone broke the silence in the car. Scott Hampton the passenger answered the call with his usual impeccable phone manner, "'Ello what do ya want?"

"It's me, how did it go, did you manage to check the place over?" the voice on the other end asked.

"Oh 'ello boss, yeh it went ok; we saw everythin' we needed to, shouldn't be any prob to sort it for Saturday." The car driver, Michael Elvis Aaron Hatton (his teenage mother had been a one time fan of the great man)[1] strained to hear the conversation over the driving rain and the roar of the car's illegal exhaust system.

The voice said, "Alright that's good, just as long as it's all in place for Saturday; is there anything else you need?" On hearing this Hatton leaned across towards the phone and said, "Tell 'im to send us another two 'undred quid, there's a few things we need to source yet." Hampton passed on the message; with a reluctant tone the voice at the other end agreed to send the money then rang off. The Fiesta entered the estate and pulled up on the car park of

---

1        Elvis Aaron Presley 1935-1977, `The King`.

the flats where the Hatton and Hampton partnership were based. They made the descent up the stairwell to the third floor flat. They had lived there long enough not to notice the acrid smell of the combined urine of dog, cat and man that pervaded the place. As long as their door was still intact when they got home all was well in the world.

\*\*\*\*\*

Just over four thousand miles and a whole lifestyle away from Victor's world, Hugo Brockleston languished on the deck of the 'Lucy B', his luxury yacht. It was just after 1pm in the Bahamas and the weather was pleasant and bright. There had been a fairly early end to that year's rainy season and the absence of the short heavy showers which characterised it meant that long relaxed lunches in the open air could now proceed uninterrupted. Hugo sat back in his chair and lovingly put a match to a large Cuban cigar; he looked across the deck and contemplated the curve of Jane Rotherby-Hyde's bottom as she dried herself following a lunchtime swim. Jane was Hugo's latest conquest, the daughter of a successful Lloyd's name, Richard Rotherby-Hyde. Rotherby-Hyde had shrewdly gone into underwriting in the aftermath of the big disaster of the early nineties. Jane seemed to possess very little of her father's business acumen, but to Hugo this was of little consequence. She knew how to live the high life and organise his social gatherings and that was all that mattered aboard the 'Lucy B'. They had met at a house party in Nassau, just after Hugo returned to the Bahamas from England following the funeral of his father. The two had become known as an 'item' in the islands shortly afterwards. They immediately became firm friends and soon after Jane moved aboard the 'Lucy B'.

"Jane old girl, what do you fancy doing this weekend? I hear Johnnie Marchington is planning a bit of a regatta over near Cat Island," Hugo shouted across to Jane. Jane slowly turned to face Hugo, smiling as usual; she let the towel fall to the deck as she walked over to him.

"Yes that sounds like fun, not seen Johnnie for months, but I hope we are not going on the island, I find it so spooky with all that spirit stuff they believe in, gives me the creeps," she said as she collapsed on the deck lounger next to him. The two lazed in the afternoon sun, sipping cold drinks, picking at the food laid out at the side of them and talking casually about the proposed schedule for the weekend. There were no other more pressing matters to spoil the air of tranquillity as the 'Lucy B' bobbed at anchor on the warm blue waters.

# *Chapter Two*

IT WAS THURSDAY MORNING, TWO days before the opening shoot. Victor woke from a disturbed sleep at 4.30am; he felt exhausted but his mind would not let his body take its much-needed rest. He had settled in his bed the night before with the old dog taking up his usual position on the floor at the bedside but sleep had not come easy if at all. His mind had turned over every possible means of sabotage that he had heard of or had been able to invent for himself. The simple fact of it was that protecting such a finely balanced set-up as a game shoot on a country estate from the destructive powers of who knows how many determined people without a small army of assistants was just about impossible. He may have been able to persuade Mowbray to have provided some part time assistance from the other estate workers but that would have meant admitting to the potential situation that was developing, so silence and vigilance was the only policy that he could come up with at the moment. He had gone over the possibility of confiding in one of the shoot's regular beaters, but had not quite come around to doing anything about it. The beater in mind was a police officer, a `traffic cop` for most of his career; but a man with a real passion for the shoot and the countryside. He had been coming to the shoot for over ten years with his dogs that were of a similar nature to old Storm, dogs that would never have been acceptable attending at the peg of a `gentleman gun` due to their unashamed enthusiasm often getting the better of them. Dogs whose very souls were one with the hunting and retrieving of game, as close as siblings to their masters and probably more valued. The man had been born on a small dairy farm in the county and grown up in the country surrounded by hunting, shooting and fishing, but rarely having the opportunity to participate due to the farm work taking priority. He had been more academically gifted than previous generations of his folk and had been away to study agriculture at university

11

in the early 1980s. The imposition of milk quotas[2] and the general downturn in the erstwhile booming dairy farming industry eventually led to him joining the Constabulary after spending a few years in agriculture. He had been originally invited along to beat at the shoot by one of the older members in an act of gratitude after he had managed to get the farmer compensation money from a travelling family whose daughter had crashed through his fence whilst drink driving. This had not gone down too well with many shoot members due to the fear of their capacity to drive home after the merriment in the shoot shed at the end of the day. One was once heard to remark, "A bloody copper, what the hell has he asked him here for, that's the last thing we want!" As the years had passed some of this prejudice had subsided, but there were still some who secretly held Constable Nick Jones at arm's length even if it was only subconsciously. Even Victor had to admit to himself that he felt uneasy at opening up completely to Nick, but he knew that perhaps the day that he had to was fast approaching.

After a token attempt at some breakfast Victor set out for the woods. He drove towards the shoot with trepidation, the dog sitting silently on the passenger seat looking contented at the thought of another day in his own private heaven, roaming the woodlands with his master. The lanes were silent and empty, save only for an odd rabbit scurrying back to the hedgerow in the glare of the Land Rover's headlights. The old 4x4 turned into a muddy gateway and headed across the sodden fields towards the Long Gorse. Victor's first intention was to check the pens and birds in this wood, as it was the heart of the shoot. As he got out of the Land Rover Victor noticed two pairs of footprints in the mud leading into and out of the small hatch that gave easy access onto the main ride that cut through the wood. They were faint due to the pounding of the overnight rain, but they were still distinctive; he could tell his old worn out Wellington boots had not made them. They looked more like training shoes of some sort. He stopped for a while and examined them closer in the light of his torch. His heart pounded and his fist clenched at the thought that he could be about to find devastation in the wood and he had been sitting at home by the

---

2        In 1984 a milk quota was imposed on British dairy farmers in an attempt to address the problem of over production, severely restricting the incomes of some of the smaller producers who were unable to afford to buy or rent extra quotas.

fire or asleep in his bed while strangers destroyed his livelihood and hard work. He hurried on through the hatch and down the ride. He rushed along the well-worn path heedless of disturbing the birds, his only thought the wire of the pens and unimaginable disturbance to the birds' habitat. When he got to the main pen he circled it like a starving fox; startled birds panicked in the torch light as he desperately checked the wire all around the enclosure. As he turned the last corner of the pen he cursed himself, realising the disturbance he was causing in his frenzied inspection. He stood in the dark silence of the wood realising he was doing as much damage as any uncaring saboteur could. Old Storm sat down by his feet, totally bemused at the sudden stillness after the frenzy. "I am bloody losing it old lad, aren't I?" he said as much to himself as to the dog. The two then walked through the rest of the wood and all the adjoining drives, until Victor was satisfied that all was well, at least for the time being anyway. At least the disturbance to the birds would have a little while to sort itself prior to the shoot day the following morning he thought to himself.

The dawn saw him topping up feed hoppers and cutting back the odd briar that had managed to creep across the rides since his last 'blitz' on them about a month ago. He began to feel better about things and the sun rising on that clear dry morning in the woods relaxed his erstwhile turbulent mind. The woods were still green, as was often the case at the start of the season; cold frosty weather that felled the briars and undergrowth had not usually come until after Christmas in recent years. The morning passed quickly and by midday he had done all that was required, he had even had time to check all the numbered pegs around the woods that marked the position of each gun on the separate drives. A few had been damaged and needed some attention or replacing, but that was not out of the ordinary, certainly nothing suspicious at all. There were always a few of the posts knocked over or small numbered plaques removed by livestock or errant kids from the village.

By about 1pm Victor was entering the 'Brockleston Arms' in the village; old Storm followed him in, his tail wagging like a clockwork toy. He knew that the rare visits to 'The Brocky', as the locals called it, meant stray crisps and bits of pie would be coming his way from all the folks who couldn't resist his sorrowful eyes. If there was anything that came a close second to being in the woods it was certainly food. The pub was quiet, as it usually was at that time of day. There was only a pair of male business types in one corner making loud animated conversation about some forthcoming meeting; and what looked like a middle aged office affair occupying the small table by the window that overlooked the green. The couple were glancing furtively around and talking quietly. She looked at least fifteen years his junior. None of my business Victor thought to himself as he bought a pint of 'Old Steamer', his favourite ale, from the bar and then settled down on the old oak settle by the bar. Storm strayed across to the business types as they had their food in front of them, but Victor gave him a stern "sit" and he reluctantly settled at his feet, the glowing fire at least some consolation.

"You 'avin' anythin' to eat love?" asked Sarah Stokes the barmaid.

"Have you got any of that hot pot you usually do?"

"Yes, just made some fresh this morning, I'll get you some," she replied. Within a few minutes Sarah was out with a bowl of the steaming food; she put it down in front of Victor and made a great fuss of arranging the cutlery she had brought, lingering that bit longer than was strictly necessary.

"There you go handsome; it's a nice bit of lamb in that." She then sat down opposite him and they talked about how the shoot was going. Sarah was always interested and was often one of the beaters when she could get time off from her duties at the pub. They talked for about a quarter of an hour, discussing dogs and characters on the shoot, there was always a bit of gossip to pass the time in Brockleston and if there wasn't Victor was sure Sarah made some up. He made no mention of his recent worries and somehow they seemed surreal in that tranquil cosy pub, chatting to Sarah like he always had. Victor had known Sarah for all his life; she was perhaps three years or so younger than him and had grown up in the village. They had only really become socially familiar in the last few years, mainly through him being a little worse for drink and losing his inhibitions when he visited the pub with some of the beaters and guns after the shoots. She had been a bit wayward in her mid twenties. Despite doing well for herself and marrying a local businessman, she had got mixed up with a crowd from Limcester and ended up experimenting with hard drugs and making up for the quiet teenage years she had spent in

Brockleston. She broke her husband's heart and eventually left him, not being seen again until she arrived back in the village in her late thirties, taking up residence in a house in a small close built by a housing trust. Despite being well-known to the police in Limcester through her past domestic issues, she was never actually convicted of anything. This was more than could have been said of some of her ex associates though, some of whom had been involved in serious crime. Despite Victor's knowledge of her past, he still liked her and considered her one of the few people in the village that he could have a meaningful conversation with. He liked to think it was not always because he had just drunk a potent mix of port and whisky in the shoot shed, followed by real ale in the 'Brocky' that they got on so well. In appearance she was not the sort of woman that Victor went for, but the whole picture was pleasing to him when coupled with her personality. Her slim long legs, always encased in close fitting jeans, and the short woollen sweater showing off the ring in her pierced navel were not really things that fitted in with the village life. There had been many evenings since Susan's death that he had wished he had the courage to call at Sarah's door, but the meetings had remained restricted to chance conversations in the pub or on the shoot. Whilst they were chatting the weather outside took a turn for the worse; the pleasant clear morning had changed to a dark grey miserable afternoon. The storm clouds had rolled in again from the hills and the rain started to beat against the pub's old window frames.

"You 'avin' another drink then? You're never going back out to the woods again in this are you Vic?" She leaned on the bar, bored with the lack of activity in the place. Victor hesitated, then decided she was probably right; he accepted another pint of ale and settled down for a bit longer; he did not really feel like repeating the soaking he had had the night before. Despite his arguments Sarah bought him the drink, he was embarrassed as he knew she must earn even less than his meagre wage. There was a little pleasure in the thought of her buying it for him even so.

By about 2.30pm the other customers had departed and there were just Victor, Sarah and Storm left in the pub. Storm was gainfully employed in searching the floor for any bits of food that had been dropped.

"Well it looks like that's it for today, there's no one else likely to be coming in now; I'm going to have an early finish, I am back in at six to open up again anyway." She then cleared up the few glasses and plates from the tables and bar.

"Good job I wasn't planning having some more. Do you want a lift home as I am passing your place, and it's raining cats and dogs again out there?" Victor said as he gathered himself together to leave. She accepted his offer and locked up the pub; the licensee Bill Stewart and his wife were away on holiday and had left Sarah in charge. They drove in silence down the lane towards the edge of the village where Sarah's house was. Victor was again dying to ask her out for an evening but could not find the words as usual.

"There you go, saved you a soaking and muddy boots anyway; are you coming along tomorrow?" Victor asked as Sarah stepped down from the Land Rover's passenger seat.

"I don't know about muddy boots, but I've got a muddy bum now thanks to your dog," she replied pointing to her jeans where she had been sitting. Victor apologised in his embarrassment, kicking himself mentally for yet another clumsy faux pas.

"Sorry, no I can't make tomorrow, I have to work as I'm in sole charge. By the way I was only teasing; see you Vic and thanks for the lift hun." With that she went off into the house and Victor drove off towards his cottage, his mind again beginning to turn over his problems now that solitude was restored.

Back in the cottage Victor could not settle. He had resolved to go back to the woods in the early hours to check that all was well. Then to stay close by to make sure it stayed that way prior to the shoot meet at Home Farm at 10am that morning. He knew he should get some sleep in the meantime, but that was easier said than done in his present state of mind He knew he had done his best for the shoot. In fact, all he could possibly do without bringing in outside help and reporting the matter to Mowbray anyway. He did eventually manage to sleep in the chair for a few hours, but it was a disturbed sleep, intertwined with images of Susan, Sarah and strange shadowy figures disturbing roosting pheasants and driving them from the woods into the night.

Victor woke at about at 11.45pm; the house was cold, the meagre fire in the hearth had long since died and the cold had come down like an icy blanket across his shoulders. He got up, shivering, and poured whisky into a tumbler; gulping it down and wincing as the stinging fluid entered his body driving away the ice demon. After picking up his shotgun, a pocketful of cartridges and his torch, he set off for the woods on foot, cursing at Storm to stop his excited panting. It had been a long time since he had walked across the fields to the shoot drives; he told himself he had got soft in using the Land Rover all the time. The moonlit march across the wet glistening fields seemed to take forever. He was actually travelling at quite a pace in his apprehensive eagerness to get to the woods to see that all was well, but he felt that his feet were made of lead and he was getting no closer to the woods. After what seemed to him like hours, he arrived at the outlying Graves Spinney and melted into the cover of the trees with Storm at his heel. Apart from the occasional hoot of an owl and call of a distant fox, no other sounds disturbed the night. There was hardly any wind, so any sound should have been easy to pick up in the stillness. That at least was something that had gone his way for once he thought. The gamekeeper continued on his patrol; he checked all the woods and pens and found to his relief that all was well; by three o' clock he was satisfied that so far the shoot had not been compromised.

*****

"What the hell where you playing at? That's just great that is getting us locked up tonight of all nights," Scott Hampton bawled at `Elvis` Hatton as they sat on the unyielding wood of the bench in a featureless police cell in Limcester nick. The two hundred pounds that had been supplied to them for essential purchases had proved too much of a temptation on a Friday night in town. They had spent it all on booze and the statutory drunken take-away which always follows a night in the pubs and clubs. That would not have been so bad if they had then set off for Brockleston in the early hours as planned. But Elvis had given into temptation and started baiting a young Constable by shouting the usual abuse at him. This was compounded by a van full of Area Support Group Officers coming around the corner at about the same time and taking exception to Elvis's tirade. The end result was that after much trading of punches and further insults, Messrs Hatton and Hampton were arrested for the first time in years. At about 7.30am a mobile phone rang in the prisoners' property lockers of the custody office; it went unanswered and an irate caller left a less than complimentary message for its owner.

✳✳✳✳✳

It was a tired and cold but optimistic Victor Drew that walked into the little cottage at around 8.30am that Saturday morning. He had completed a long and lonely vigil in the woods but his mind for once was settled and he was looking forward to the opening shoot. He was whistling as he showered and put on his tidy clothes for the day's event; he even felt like eating a decent breakfast for a change. Even old Storm was treated to a bowl full of food to sustain him through the hard day's work ahead. The Brockleston Keeper set off to the shoot meet at 9.30am, at about the same time as two miscreants were leaving Limcester Central Police Station carrying charge and bail forms and suffering from hangovers.

# Chapter Three

VICTOR PULLED INTO THE YARD at Home Farm just as Mowbray was getting out of his own vehicle. He had intended arriving before the agent but Mowbray had just beaten him to it. The only other vehicle that had arrived was that of Nick Jones who was usually early. Nick was in the corner of the yard exercising his two Labradors after the drive from the neighbouring parish of Brocklesby, a sparsely populated area consisting of a few houses and farms spread over a large area that could not really be called a village. Before Victor had a chance to speak to Nick, Mowbray was at the door of the Land Rover.

"Ah Drew, there you are, come on man, we need to get inside and finalise the day's drives; there's a lot hanging on today's shoot." Victor followed Mowbray around the side of the building and into the shoot shed. The early morning sun was streaming in through the dirty windows, showing up the dust and mouse droppings on the tables. It had been usual for Mowbray to have the shed cleaned and tidied by some of the estate staff for the opening shoot but he did not seem to have bothered this year. Victor cursed to himself and thought that he would have done it himself if he had known it had been left in the state it was in; too late for that now. Mowbray brushed the dust off a table that ran along the window side of the room and threw down a pile of flip chart sheets that he had been carrying. There were diagrams drawn in marker pen of all the woods and drives on the shoot with instructions on the direction of the beaters and positions of the guns for each drive.

"I thought we would be a bit better organised this year; I know that some of the old shoot members are a bit past it and get confused and there're always new guests each year that need to see the layout. These will show them exactly what's going on and help things run a bit smoother, all being well. I want you to use them on your briefing. Here's the order of the day, so put the charts up on the hooks here on the wall and we are all ready." Mowbray used the hustling overbearing tone that he usually adopted when he was giving Victor instructions.

Victor set about the task of hanging up Mowbray's diagrams in the order of the drives for the day. He thought they looked like some bizarre clues for a treasure hunt but he said nothing and did as he was told. The Mowbrays of this world were best not met head on, especially if there may be trouble around the corner that would play into their hands. Mowbray went back outside, leaving Victor at his task. Nick Jones then entered the shed along with a couple of other beaters. Victor apologised to Nick for not getting the chance to speak outside and welcomed the three to the shoot. Good beaters were not easy to come by, especially at Brockleston where they were not paid. Despite Victor's appeals to Mowbray over the years, the beaters had to make do with a bit of lunch, and a few drinks at the end of the day. They also got a bird or two to take home when the day's bag and the shoot captain's mood allowed. This was never an issue with the regular beaters though; they came because they loved it, so in that these things were never an issue. Victor did manage to thank them all once a year by inviting them to shoot on the beaters' day at the end of the season and providing them with drinks and some food at the 'Brockleston Arms' afterwards. These were often the most memorable and enjoyable days. They were even better when Susan was around; she would come beating too and would always insist on everyone coming back for food at the cottage. She would often be up half the night before the beaters' day, just preparing things. The shoot was far less formal than it had been in his grandfather's time. Beaters and guns now shared the same shed and there was at least some conversation between them. There was still a bit of a divide though, with some of the guns still keeping the beaters at arm's length and the beaters and guns sitting at opposite sides of the room. In the old days all the guns had been the guests of the late Lord Brockleston and had been wined and dined at the hall. The beaters were mainly estate employees and had to eat their food in the woods or whilst walking between the drives, the keepers being slightly better off in dining at cook's table in the kitchen, resplendent in their green velveteen garb.

The members and their guests for the day started to arrive in the shed; Mowbray also came back in after meeting them in the yard. There were a dozen members of the shoot and each week six of them invited a guest when it was their turn to do so. Mowbray rarely joined the guns; a member would occasionally ask him as a guest during the season and he sometimes accepted. But he was not really a shooting man, if a countryman at all. His main interest in the guns was their pockets. He usually left Victor and that season's shoot captain to organise the season. Victor felt it was typical of his luck that Mowbray had taken a suddenly increased interest in proceedings.

The shed was back to how it should be. There was the hum of genial conversation. Stories, jokes and anecdotes were being related and those that had not seen each other since the previous January were catching up on matters. Victor circulated, handing out the day's shoot cards to the guns, each one drawing one from the fan of cards in Victor's hand then looking to see who they were alongside on the first drive. Flasks of steaming coffee were opened and passed around along with the odd hip flask of more substantial liquid. It was the turn of Robbie Langdon, a local farmer of nearly retirement age, to be the shoot captain for the season. Robbie was ill at ease at the prospect of blowing the horn and summoning everyone's attention from their reverie. He eventually managed to blow the squeaky little silver horn that hung around his neck and called the gathering to order. He quickly gave the usual safety briefing to the guns regarding the angle of their shots, the safe use and carriage of shotguns and that no ground game such as rabbits and hares was to be shot. Victor then proceeded to go through the order of the drives for the morning, starting with the duck drive at Brockleston Pits, then onto Lady Jane's Moss and Old Jack's Slang before visiting Graves Spinney and then back to the shoot shed for the usual lunch of hot pot that had been prepared at `The Brocky`. He had to admit to himself that Mowbray's diagrams were actually useful and he took the trouble to acknowledge this at the end of the briefing, thanking him in front of all that were assembled. After all it did no harm to at least attempt to be on the right side of the agent. Nick Jones standing towards the back of the shed felt a jab in his back and turned to receive a wry smile and a wink from Harry Black, another of the old beating hands; he knew what Victor said about Mowbray in his more outspoken moments in the pub.

The assembled group filed out of the shed and went to the varied collection of transport assembled at the farm. There were four wheel drives both old and new, vans, estate cars and some saloons with blankets on their backseats in a vain attempt to protect the upholstery from the muddy paws of their canine passengers. Excited dogs were let out of the vehicles and they raced around the yard anticipating the sport ahead. There was a noisy commotion as the handlers of Labradors, Spaniels and even the odd Jack Russell got their charges under control. There weren't too many dogs at Brockleston that would do well in obedience and gun dog trials. The first drive at Brockleston Pits was within a short walk of the shoot shed. The party made their way past the vehicles and over a small stile at the back of the yard. The two pits set in a gently sloping pasture field had ducks introduced on them the previous summer to create some variety in the game on the shoot. Previously the sport had only been provided by the pheasants released in the woods and what happened to come along in the form of wild duck and woodcock. There had been partridges many years before but not in Victor's time; modern farming methods had now made the area unsuitable. Victor told Robbie to get his guns into position quickly and quietly and to instruct them that they were `live on their pegs`, that is, they were to fire as soon as any ducks came over them and not to wait for Robbie's whistle to sound. He held the beaters back by the stile; the ducks were easily disturbed and he did not want them flying before the guns were ready. Once the guns were in position the beaters with dogs made their way to positions behind them ready to pick up shot game. There was no need for beaters at the pits, Victor and Storm would be all that was required to get the ducks into the air. There was a loud cry of "Over!" and the first flurry of ducks was airborne, gaining height rapidly as they flew towards the farm buildings and over guns 2, 3, 4 and 5, the rapidly beating wings whistling in the still morning air. The guns were ready and five Mallards fell from the sky, bouncing on the still hard pasture. Victor marked where they fell as he shouted at Storm to stop him going off to retrieve the shot game. The first flurry must have contained the best part of 30 ducks and the next one of similar size followed shortly after. Fortunately they went to the right of the first flight and not over the empty guns. The guns that were at the Brockleston Hall side of the pits were treated to some good shooting this time and another nine ducks were added to the bag. A final and much smaller flurry of birds then got up and flew over guns 6 to 9 where a further three birds were consigned to the bag. The captain sounded the horn to mark the end of the drive; enough ducks had been shot for the first day and he wanted them to last well into the season. The shot birds that had not been retrieved during the drive were quickly found by the dogs and all the ducks were carried back to the shoot shed to be hung on the game racks. Victor's venture with the ducks could not have gone better; usually only a fraction of the guns would have suitable birds over them or the ducks would be spooked prior to them being ready to take the shot. Robbie Langdon was smiling; he could be heard singing the gamekeeper's praises all across the yard. Even Mowbray said, "Well done Drew, let's hope the rest of the day is as good," as they went to the vehicles prior to setting off on the short drive down the road through the village to 'Lady Jane's Moss' or 'The Moss' as it was more commonly known.

At 'The Moss' the vehicles were parked on the roadside and the guns made their way to their positions shepherded by Robbie Langdon, whilst Victor and the beaters walked to the end of the wood furthest from the village. On the way across Victor asked Nick Jones to take his two dogs to the opposite end of the wood to pick up shot birds as the guns on that side had not got any of their own dogs with them. He also sent Harry Black along with Nick for Harry to act as a `stop`[3] at that end of the wood to prevent pheasants running out towards the guns. Victor also knew Nick and Harry were old friends and that they would enjoy the walk and the chance to catch up socially. The whistle blew and the beaters that had lined out at the end of the wood climbed over the fence and entered the autumn tinted calmness of the tree canopy. Victor was in the centre of the line directing operations, keeping an eye on the line and its pace and any over enthusiastic dogs that got too far forward. The sound of sticks hitting tree trunks and undergrowth merged with the excited yelps of spaniels who had scented their quarry. Beaters shouted and whistled their dogs back and every so often there

---

3    A beater positioned to prevent birds running from a cover before taking flight or before the guns are in position.

were shouts of "Over", "Forward", "Back", "Left" or "Right" and other variations, forewarning the guns of an approaching bird put up by the beaters or their dogs. To Victor's delight these shouts started very soon after their entry into the wood and were kept up regularly as the line progressed through the wood. The sound of shotguns firing at the flying game was almost continuous and he knew this was the hallmark of a good drive. Storm was working just a few yards ahead of Victor; there was a brown flash just by the dog's nose and something that looked like a large brown-flecked bat took to the air. It made its way forward, jinking between the trees. Victor shouted "Woodcock Forward!" A few seconds later there was a frenzied flurry of shots at the far end of the wood.

The beating line reached the end of the wood and the dogs emerged into the field with the guns. Victor shouted to Robbie that the line was through the wood and the captain blew the horn to signify the end of the drive. As Victor emerged from the tree line, he was met by a beaming Nick Jones who was carrying three brace of pheasants and the woodcock that had gone forward. Nick was praising one of his two dogs and was obviously pleased with young 'Teddy', the yellow Labrador. The birds that had been cleanly shot and three that had been wounded and run into a nearby hedge were picked up. The bag from this wood alone looked like it was in the region of fifteen brace.[4] The day was still going well. The party made its way back to the vehicles and set off through a gateway and across the fields for Old Jack's Slang, a long narrow strip of trees in a slight valley running along the boundary between two fields not far from 'The Moss', often a place where pheasants strayed to from the nearby woods and it provided good shelter when the weather was bad. Victor had planted a small game crop in a corner of one of the fields at the top end of the Slang. This had increased its capability of holding game.

The convoy of vehicles made its way across the fields like some strange forgotten army still looking for a war it could not find. This image was enhanced by an old ex army long wheel base Land Rover that carried the majority of the beaters, its rear packed with men and wet muddy dogs that were attempting to climb all over them. All was as it should be thought Victor as he leaned back and

---

4    A sporting or country term for two or a pair.

relaxed in the front passenger seat of Robbie Langdon's Nissan Pickup which also carried the balance of the beaters seated on some damp straw bales in the rear.

At 12.30pm the last bird was picked up at Graves Spinney and the vehicles headed back towards the village and the shoot shed. Robbie and Victor dropped out of the column as it passed the pub to collect the big pan of hot pot for lunch. Sarah met them at the back door with the pan and asked how it had gone. Victor tried not to sound too excited but let her know that it had gone well. He thanked her and said that he would be back in the evening with the pan. The shed was buzzing with conversation when Victor and Robbie arrived. The noise level only subsided slightly as the hot pot was distributed and packs of bread rolls and jars of pickled red cabbage were passed around. Victor ran a quick eye over the game racks; there were 17 ducks, 51 pheasants and 2 woodcock hanging up. There had been days when the total bag had been far less than this half-time account he thought. Victor looked around to catch Mowbray's eye, but he could not see the agent in the shed. He asked Phillip Boddington, a retired farmer, ex shoot member and now beater, where Mowbray was. Phillip always new everything as he made it his business to.

"Oh he went off somewhere in a right hurry as soon as we got back in the yard; he looked none too pleased with something, not seen him since," said Phillip as he ladled another pile of red cabbage on top of his steaming bowl of hot pot. Well best not to gloat thought Victor and settled down to enjoy his hot food with the agreeable company. It wasn't unusual for Mowbray to have more important things to take care of than the shoot. After about 45 minutes Robbie Langdon drew the group to order again and Victor made his second speech of the day, outlining the afternoon drives. Hall Wood which was only a short drive from the shed and situated at the rear of Brockleston Hall was to host the sport for the second half of the day. This had been the centre piece of the estate's sporting activities ever since the first birds were released at Brockleston many years ago. It had gone into a decline with grown up rides and dilapidated release pens over recent years, but Victor had spent the last twelve months bringing the wood back into line and he had high hopes for it this season.

Two lengthy drives were the plan for the afternoon, using the two rides that ran through the 60 acre wood. He had to add some details to Mowbray's maps as the agent was not as up to date with the wood as Victor was.

Just before 1.30pm the group was on the move again and shortly after the guns were positioned along the first of the two rides. The first drive was as good as Victor hoped and good sport was shown again. The second drive sometime later was equally good and the day ended on a high note with a further brace of woodcock being added to the bag. Unfortunately not `a left and a right`5 by the same gun, but very welcome in any case and a rare sight at Brockleston in recent years for some reason, the woodcock being a migratory wild bird and its presence or otherwise on the shoot being largely a matter of chance.

By 4pm the vehicles were back in the yard and having their windows steamed up by damp exhausted dogs that were settling down for a well earned rest inside them. The human contingent of the shoot trooped into the shed like a conquering army. Those carrying birds hung the game on the racks and picked up a glass of port or whisky from the end of the table where Robbie Langdon was cheerfully pouring them out. Victor had a quick count up of the bag when the last birds had been brought in; he was amazed to see there were 120 pheasants, 22 duck and 4 woodcock. He could not remember having such a bag in his time as keeper. He decided to set to and tie the birds into braces; as there were so many he got Nick and Harry to help him and the task was completed fairly quickly. All three then settled down at the top right-hand corner of the table to enjoy the drink and talk that was flowing freely. David Radford, local farmer and longstanding member of the shoot, struck the side of a glass with a spoon and called for quiet. It was that time of the proceedings again; all fell silent waiting for him to speak. This was another highlight of the day, when David produced the little notebook that he used to record all the numbers that the party gave him in the morning in an attempt to guess the size of the day's bag. A couple of pounds were wagered to win £25; the rest would go into the fund to help buy the port, whisky and beer for the shoot.

---

5    Shooting a pair of birds in quick succession without reloading, using both barrels of a shotgun.

David made a big show of thanking Victor and the beaters for an excellent day, then went on to announce the winner; it was Harry who was the closest as he had put the highest number down; even so he was 20 below the actual total. He received his winnings from David then added his name and the date to the list scribbled on the back wall of the shed before sitting back down with his glass of port. Shortly after people started to leave, so Victor took up his customary position by the game racks next to the door and handed out the braces of game as they left, saying goodnight and wishing them a safe journey home. The handshakes of the guests and some of the guns were loaded with some healthy tips in appreciation of a good day's sport at Brockleston. He had taken the trouble to remove the `pin feathers`[6] from the wings of the woodcocks and made sure those that had shot them were presented with these in one of the little brown envelopes that he always carried in his pocket on shoot days for that purpose. They were also offered the opportunity of taking the bird home; he would not give them out automatically as some of the guns did not really want to take them in recent years, not really appreciating the delicacy or knowing how to prepare it. There was eventually only the usual diehard few remaining in the shed – Nick Jones, Robbie Langdon, Andrew Probert, Charlie Davidson and his guest for the day, Bob Stephenson, who was a Magistrate in the adjoining county. They tidied up the shed, washing the glasses and the pan from the pub, and then stowing things away in the big old lockable wooden cupboard in the corner. The group then left the shed and headed for the village pub in a convoy of vehicles escorting the infamous pan back to its home.

'The Brocky' was almost empty, as was often the case at that time of the year. Only old George Needham was there, propping up the end of the bar by the door and chatting to Sarah, who was polishing glasses behind the bar. George was there at that time every evening; he drove the five miles from his own village, just to have his two pints of mild ale and look longingly at Sarah who always played him along. The group entered the pub in their stockinged feet; they had left their boots in the porch, as they knew that the mud would not have gone down too well on the carpets that Bill Stewart had

---

6    The tiny feathers located by the central joint of a woodcock's wing, one on each wing. Much prized as trophies by shooters ('feather in the cap') and also by artists for painting intricate work such as miniature portraits or landscapes etc.

fitted when he moved in. This was always a source of annoyance as previously there had just been the old stone floor and dogs were allowed in the pub to dry out by the big fire.

"Hiya, how did it go today Vic?" asked Sarah.

"Absolutely fantastic, couldn't have been better, I will have trouble matching it again, that's the problem," Victor replied as he sat down on a barstool opposite her. Victor asked what they were all drinking but Charlie would have none of it, insisting that Victor would not be paying for anything. The drinks flowed and the group talked about the day; they ended up standing around a small tall table just in front of the fire. Victor had now dismissed the threatening note and was relaxing in the good company, enjoying his moment of celebration of a job well done and the luck that was always needed to provide a good day on even the best run shoots. They had all had just that bit too much to drink, but out in the dark, cold emptiness of the countryside they were more than happy circling around the bright welcoming flame that was the 'Brockleston Arms'. When Bob Stephenson discovered what Nick did for a living, he could not help relating a few amusing anecdotes about his time on the bench. This renewed impetus in the conversation passed another couple of hours and it was beyond closing time when they eventually called it a good day's sport and left for home, parting with as much regard as any man could have for another.

Sarah put the towels over the pumps and turned off the lights in the pub; she felt very alone in the sudden silence. She also felt a bit put out at Victor; he had not said a great deal to her and had been wrapped up in his group all evening. It hadn't helped that he had not even come to the bar to buy a round of drinks. She walked down the lane towards her home. She cursed at not getting a lift from Victor; she had worked hard all evening serving them then they had just disappeared into the night. As she turned into the close she saw that there was a light on in the front room of her house; she swore to herself for leaving it on, she could hardly cope with her bills as it was. What she did not notice was the dark coloured Ford Fiesta parked in the lane just beyond the entrance to the close. As Sarah got to her door, she thought she could hear voices from inside the house, but dismissed this immediately. Then as she went to put her key in the lock the door swung open and she saw that it had been forced. She went into the front room to be confronted by the sight of two people the like of whom she hoped never to see again. Elvis and Scott were reclining on her two small sofas either side of the room as if they owned the place. They both had cans of cheap lager in their hands and her carpet was decorated with several empty cans and the remains of two takeaway kebabs.

"Hello Sarah love, missed your pretty face and tight arse these last twelve months. So this is where you've been hidin'; out 'ere with all the hoorays an' their pet halfwits," said Elvis in a menacing tone. There was some purpose to their visit; she knew them too well to think it was a pleasant late night social call. She froze in total shock for a few seconds, her heart pounding.

"How the hell did you find me? What do you want coming here at this time of night?" she blurted out before thinking and immediately regretted it, remembering what the two were capable of; she had seen their handiwork first hand in the past. Before the words died on her lips Scott was up on his feet; he gave her an almighty slap across the side of her head, nearly knocking her over, then pushed her down onto the sofa he had vacated.

"Now then bitch, I thought you'd know better than to welcome your old friends like that; as a matter of fact we are here for a little chat. It's amazing who you can find when you have a bit of cash to flash and you have the right contacts." Elvis spat the words out like venom itself. It was obvious there was to be no catching up with social pleasantries. The right side of Sarah's head throbbed from the force of the blow and she could hardly hear on that side, but she was listening hard enough. It was information they wanted; information on Victor's habits and movements, especially for the past evening. Reluctantly she told them what she knew of Victor's activities. She tried to gloss over it, but they knew she was looking after the pub and that she was on friendly terms with him. Whatever their interest in Victor was, it was not worth the risk of getting another slap, one had been quite enough. They would not accept that her relationship with Victor was as low key as she claimed and refused to believe that she only knew about his movements on shoot days and his occasional visits to the pub. The further assault that she had tried to avoid was not long in coming. Elvis got to his feet and grabbed her by the hair, slamming her face into the small table at the side of the sofa with so much force that its flimsy legs snapped and splintered. Her head was yanked up again to receive a left fist in the nose and she was then thrown to the floor and kicked several times on her back and legs by both of them. The two then left the house without a word. She was left lying face down on the carpet that she had so carefully looked after since moving into the house; the carpet that was now decorated with a cocktail of spilt beer, greasy kebab meat and blood. She lay sobbing in severe pain for what must have been half an hour; she half expected one of the neighbours to appear to see what had happened but no one came. No doubt they had heard the noise from the house and decided not to get involved. Sarah was still viewed as an outsider with a past and they did not want to get involved or at least be seen to be doing so. There had been comments made about Victor being on social terms with her. It was something that was still not accepted by some as `the done thing`.

The cold dampness of the night drifting in through the open door eventually brought Sarah out of her tortured incapacity and she struggled to her feet, wincing at the pain she felt all over her body and wiping the blood from her face. She closed the front door and secured it as best she could. The frame was split where the tang of the lock went into it, but it would at least stay closed for the time being and there was a security chain which gave at least some protection whilst she was at home. She looked at the state of the lounge and burst into tears again; they had done a good job on her both physically and emotionally. If they had raped her she couldn't have felt more defiled. A murky past that she thought had been left behind had suddenly appeared in her own home, as violent and horrible as it ever was. Her head was not only hurting due to the assault; it also ached with the effort of wondering what to do. She did not want the Police at her door fuelling the neighbours' distrust of her and she did not want to tell Victor about the visit for fear of revealing too much of her past to him. She doubted that he would understand too much of it. She picked up the telephone receiver, more in contemplation than direct decision, but found the decision had been made for her, at least for the time being. The line was dead; the wires had been torn from the wall and were lying next to the broken junction box by the base of the curtains. She had the most painful shower that she had taken in years, swallowed six Paracetamol tablets that she found in the kitchen drawer, drank what was left of a bottle of wine that was left in the fridge door and went to bed. The vile pus from the great festering incurable sore that was the Brandley Estate had leaked into her life again and she felt despair like she had never done before.

# *Chapter Four*

I<small>T WAS ABOUT</small> 9.30<small>AM WHEN</small> Victor awoke the following morning. Intense sunlight was burning through the faded curtains of the room and Storm was pawing at his arm. "Well look at the state of me, sorry old lad," he said to the old dog as he dragged himself out of bed, already feeling guilty at the thought of his celebratory lie-in. He threw on his working clothes and went downstairs to let Storm out into the yard. The old dog impatiently pushed his way out of the door before it could be opened fully and rushed outside. Victor went to the kitchen and started to make himself a drink, not giving the old dog another thought. He knew he would be back at the door in a few minutes scratching to come back inside. He did not wander far these days. The kettle started to boil on the cooker and soon Victor was sitting at the kitchen table quietly contemplating how well yesterday's opening shoot had gone. He doubted that even the critical gaze of Mowbray could find too much at fault and the guns and guests had been more than satisfied. He had started to think that the letter had been from a `crank` after all. He was suddenly disturbed by the sound of barking from outside; he looked out of the window expecting to see Storm taking exception to some passing walkers out for a Sunday morning stroll in the countryside. He could not see anyone passing in the lane but he went out and called the dog in anyway; the loud barking was a bit too much to bear with his current headache. There was always a price to pay for excess no matter how justified it felt at the time, he thought to himself. After a second cup of coffee he managed to feel well enough to get himself out of the house and set off on foot down the lane. He decided he needed a long walk to clear his head and combining this with a tour of the shoot to check all was well and top up any feed hoppers that were running low seemed like a good idea. He made his way towards Graves Spinney across the fields. As he approached the wood the bells of St Johns, the Brockleston

Parish Church, started to ring and he could see cars approaching the church down Church Lane which ran towards it. The lane only ran to the church and the surrounding farmland and was not a through road. It had been a route to the church for hundreds of years and its original users were long dead. Local folklore had it that many of them were lying beneath the soil and ancient roots of the trees in Graves Spinney. The wood was situated a short distance from the present churchyard which made the old story highly credible. Not the most comforting piece of local history to recall when visiting the woods alone during the hours of darkness. He had never witnessed anything unusual there himself but there were always those that liked to tell ghost stories in the pub to get the attention of strangers who might buy them a drink or two. When he reached the edge of the spinney he noticed that the barbed wire of the boundary fence appeared slacker than it was the last time he saw it and there were also some fragments of red material clinging to one of the barbs on the top strand. A fairly insignificant observation in itself, the cloth could have been from the clothing of kids from the village visiting the woods or passing ramblers straying from the footpath. It would have been far more alarming to him a couple of days earlier when he was worrying about having the opening shoot sabotaged. On walking through the wood nothing appeared unusual. He topped up the hoppers with some of the bags of grain that were stored in the wood, more for the sake of doing so because he was already there; it was really unnecessary as they were still fairly full in any case. The disturbance caused by the beaters the day before had not dispersed the birds too far and most were back in the wood around the feeders. He continued his trek across the drives on that side of the Brockleston Road with a similar pattern being repeated in the other woods. He eventually reached the end of 'The Moss' and came onto the lane, where he headed back towards the village. By the time he reached the 'Brockleston Arms' his hangover had gone and it had been replaced by hunger; it was about 2pm and he thought he would get a sandwich at the pub. It would also give him the opportunity of speaking to Sarah. His time in the woods had brought a realisation of how he had paid very little attention to her the night before and he was feeling a bit guilty about it. To his surprise the pub door was locked when he tried to go inside. He went to the window and peered in. The towels were over the pumps and there were no lights on behind the bar. The centre of the village was deserted; there was no reason for anyone to linger there with the pub closed. Sunday lunchtime and afternoon was the main money earner for 'The Brocky' during the winter months so its being closed at that time was very odd. He headed off towards his cottage, wondering if he had anything in the house to eat. He wasn't the best of housekeepers and there tended to be either a feast or a famine at Keeper's Cottage. As he passed the end of Sarah's close he hesitated; he wanted to call and see her and the pub being closed would have been an ideal excuse. But as usual he could not bring himself to walk into the close and knock on her door, so he carried on towards home with Storm now trailing behind. The long walk had been a bit much for the old dog following the previous day's hard work on the shoot. His arthritic hips were feeling the strain of it all. Victor slowed up in sympathy for his old friend despite his urgency to get home and eat. He knew that the old dog would follow him anywhere as long as he could drag himself along and no pain or exhaustion would stop him. Back at the cottage Victor found there were at least the makings of a simple meal and he had a plate of bacon and eggs before settling down in the chair by the fire, where he slept for the next four hours with Storm lying by his feet.

The telephone rang in the cottage, breaking the intense silence of the quiet Sunday evening and abruptly waking Victor from his sleep. Half awake, he got out of the chair and picked up the receiver. For several seconds there was silence, then a voice he barely recognised spoke softly to him. It was Sarah Stokes; she sounded drunk, far drunker than he had been the night before and she was crying. It was hard to make out what she was saying. He made out the words, "I thought it was all behind me, I had a new life here," then the phone went dead. He stood holding the receiver; he was still working out what time of day it was as he had not had a chance to wake up properly. It was some seconds before he was able to think straight. Had he imagined the call? It was certainly odd; she had never rung him before. He fed Storm and cleared the table from lunchtime, all the time turning over in his mind what Sarah had said on the phone. He could not settle and the long sleep in the chair had made him restless. He tidied himself up and drove to the 'Brockleston Arms' to see if it was open and if Sarah was there. When he walked into the pub he was greeted by Bill Stewart who had returned late that afternoon and opened up for the evening. There were just a few locals in the pub and Bill was not busy. He greeted him and asked how the shoot was going; he was always interested as it brought in a fair bit of money during the winter months. Victor told him about how well Saturday had gone then enquired about Sarah. He told Bill that the pub had been shut earlier and Bill remarked that it explained why there was so little in the till for the day and why the place was so clean and tidy. He had not seen Sarah but thought nothing of it as she always had Sunday nights off in any case. Victor said nothing about the strange phone call; he wasn't even sure he had received it in any case. He drank a pint of 'Old Steamer' whilst he was talking to Bill before making his excuses and leaving the pub. He walked back to his vehicle and sat in it for several minutes in the car park of the pub. He was turning it all over in his head again, torn between the possibility of visiting Sarah out of the blue with no good excuse or ignoring a plea for help from someone he knew. He was conscious that people would notice if he sat there too long which also added to the pressure on him. For once he made a decision; he was going round there, he would not be able to settle if he didn't. He drove into the close and parked up outside the house, he was still feeling awkward but he was determined to find out what if anything had happened. He went to the door and knocked; for several seconds there was no reply, then the door was opened with the chain still on. Sarah peered through the gap and saw who was at the door; she closed it again and then opened it, having released the chain. Victor could hardly believe what he saw. Her nose was black and swollen, she had two black eyes and her lip was split. He then understood why the pub had not been open earlier.

"My God, what's happened to you? Were you attacked walking home last night?"

"Come in before the neighbours see me." Sarah almost dragged him into the house and closed the door. Her speech was still slurred but he heard and understood this time. She told him to sit down. The room had been tidied but the carpet still looked terrible; even his limited detection skills led him to understand that whatever had happened to her had occurred in the room.

"I shouldn't have rung you, it was a mistake, sorry, we hardly know each other."

"That's alright, but what's gone on? Have you called the

police?"

"No and I'm not going to either, there's enough folks know about this as it is." Victor persisted with trying to find out what had happened, but she was clearly not going to tell him too much. She then told him that it was him these people were after and they wanted to know about his movements. She would not say who they were but warned him that they were dangerous. He could see that for himself; he wished they were back in the room too. He was also angry with himself for not thinking of her the night before and giving her a lift home. The note had some significance then; there was someone out to cause him problems and for some reason Sarah had ended up the first casualty. For the first time in years his emotions took control of him and he moved across the room and sat next to Sarah, putting his arm across her shoulders; the importance of the shoot and his job suddenly faded in the light of her injuries and distress. He looked around the room; she had got it really nice, and it was a far cry from the run down state that Keeper's Cottage had got into over the last few years. Despite the horrendous mess on the carpet he could tell it had been spotless before whatever had happened the night before. He could not imagine the violence that had taken place in the room just hours before. In a rare moment of decisiveness he said to her, "Come on, Miss Stokes, get a few things together, you are coming back with me." He expected a flat refusal or argument, but nothing was said. She sat there for a few seconds then went upstairs, coming back down again a few minutes later with a green canvas holdall. She missed her footing on the last step, nearly falling into the room and dropping the bag. Victor picked up the bag and carried it out. Sarah followed him without a word, and he helped her into the Discovery, putting the bag on the back seat. The neighbours in the close would certainly not be short of things to talk about later he thought, glancing at the state of Sarah's face. They drove in silence back to the cottage, Victor feeling suddenly awkward, but knowing that he could not have left her where she was. He got her into the cottage and sat her down; Storm was thrilled at the sight of a visitor and made the usual fuss.

"Just leave her for a bit Storm, she's not quite up to it now lad. The old dog settled at her feet, stretching out across the rug. Victor put Sarah's bag down in the hall and did what folks always do in awkward situations. He went and made some tea. She broke into a smile and half laughed when he returned.

"You're nothing if not predictable," she joked.

"Thanks for this Vic, it wasn't expected of you." The effects of the alcohol were starting to wear off. They sat and made awkward conversation for a while, then she asked him why they would want to know about him and had he been involved in anything lately. He showed her the note and said that he had dismissed it when the first shoot had ended up going well. In her own mind she could not associate her attackers with any form of animal rights activity; they were thugs and nothing more. They hardly cared for themselves let alone a few pheasants. Someone must have hired them, but she kept this to herself, just like Victor was doing with Mowbray and everyone else apart from Sarah. So far the policy had worked but now he was as worried as ever and not just for the shoot. The only thing he could do was carry on as before with his patrols, but he now realised that he wasn't just dealing with some peaceful protestors and he would really have to be on his guard. It had got to 10.30pm and he started to feel uneasy already, but he decided to wait until the early hours before venturing out onto the shoot again. He showed her around the house and told her to make herself at home; the spare room was fairly tidy if a little damp due to being closed up for so long. The small lounge and kitchen were all that there was downstairs, so the tour was fairly brief. She took a bath and went to bed at about 11.30pm and that was the last he saw of her that night.

The fire in the grate had faded to just a few scattered patches of red amongst dull grey wood ash. The log basket was empty and already the chill of the night had started to reclaim the room. It was time to go to the woods. Victor closed the cottage door, locking it behind him. The clock in the hall sounded 1am accompanied by the frustrated whining of an ageing Labrador. For the first time in 11 years Storm had been left behind by Victor. The moon was up and the countryside looked surreal, bathed in white ghostly light with the trees standing out in stark relief. There was no frost but it was only half a degree or so above freezing. There was not even the hint of a breeze. It was one of those nights when the slightest of sounds would carry for miles. He stood for a few seconds at the side of the Discovery. He was not in the mood for a long walk, but he did not want his approach heard by any that may be out there in the night. The decision made, he got in and started the engine, its coming to life not being as easy as usual due to the cold, and the noise being that bit louder too. He drove out of the gateway and turned towards the village. As he passed the pub a car passed him in the opposite direction. He could not make any details out as its headlights were full on and the driver did not bother to dip them at any point. Victor assumed it was just a late night drinker heading home through the country lanes to avoid any unwanted police attention. He made a tour of the lanes, looking for any vehicles parked out near the woods or gateways that had been freshly disturbed. The dew had formed on the grass and any footprints or tyre tracks would have shown up in the moonlight. After passing 'The Moss' and checking the lane for about two miles beyond, he turned and headed back towards Brockleston. He was satisfied that nobody had gone towards the woods from that direction. He then drove out to Home Farm, checking The Hall Wood and Brockleston Pits before driving through the yard to see if the shoot shed was secure; his final patrol was up at Graves Spinney. He parked the Land Rover by the church, walked through the graveyard and across the field to the wood. If he was ever going to meet a supernatural being then this would be the night, he thought to himself. He was not a believer in such things, but the sound of the owls and foxes echoing across the empty fields as he approached the wood did cause him to shudder at one point. He had seen nothing on his patrol, but then again he had not been silent in his approach. Prevention was no bad thing he thought. If he could keep whoever it was away from the woods he would be achieving his end. He got back to the cottage at around 2.30am; Storm welcomed him home. As usual the old dog bore no malice at the terrible insult he had just been dealt by his master. Victor went straight up to bed to make use of what was left of the night. He had decided that he would have a trip out later that day.

At 7.30am Victor was dressed and in the kitchen, cooking himself an early breakfast. To his surprise Sarah appeared down the stairs as he was putting it out on the plate.

"You're looking a bit better, want some breakfast?"

"No thanks, bit early for me, some of that coffee will be fine." The marks of the beating were still very visible but she had managed to tone them down with a liberal application of make-up. Victor asked how she had slept. Her night had passed alright apart from the hour and a half of squeaking and whining provided by Storm as he waited by the front door for Victor's return. She announced that she would be going to the pub to open up for lunchtime as normal. Victor knew that it was of no use protesting and offered her a lift as he was going to be passing on his way to where he was going that morning. This was accepted without question. At 8.30am Victor pulled up outside 'The Brocky' to drop Sarah off. After opening the door she leaned back across towards him and kissed him on the lips, to his surprise and embarrassment.

"Thanks Vic, I can't tell you how much you helped me out last night." She then walked off into the pub. He looked around to see if there was anyone around. He saw nobody but was still not at ease. There were times when village life was a bit too claustrophobic.

Victor headed out of Brockleston past 'The Moss' and on towards the border with the next county. He was off to see an old friend of his late Father's who had been a keeper for a neighbouring estate some 23 years ago. He was the last head keeper there as he had taken early retirement when the estate was sold off by its owners to pay death duties. The woods where the pheasants were released were now just a scenic back drop to a luxury housing estate and exclusive golf course. More money than could have ever been imagined by the old family that had lived there had been generated by the development. Victor tried to put this thought to the back of his mind as he entered the sheltered retirement complex close to the entrance of the main estate. In one corner of the development was the little flat now occupied by Bill Flemming, the man Victor had come to visit. Bill was standing in the little patch of garden at the front of his flat, still upright despite his 80 plus years on the planet. He was dressed in an old pair of moleskin breeks and a waxed jacket. Victor could not believe the sight before him. How out of time and place Bill looked. Like some sort of bizarre sketch from a comedy series, he thought. It cheered Victor's spirits to see Bill though. The old man recognised Victor straight away; there was nothing of the amnesia of age about Bill Flemming.

"Well if it isn't Dusty Drew's lad. Come on in son, you're the first proper visitor I've had for twelve months." Bill's delight was obvious and soon Victor and Storm were sitting in the lounge of the flat. Pets were not allowed at 'Longacre Meadows' but Bill insisted on Victor bringing the dog inside. Storm was quickly lying at Bill's feet, not needing to be asked twice. Victor looked around in disbelief as Bill went off to make tea. It was like sitting in a keeper's hut in suburbia. There were all the items of the keeper's craft and Bill's former life heaped around the floor and walls. In pride of place over what should have been the fireplace was an old photograph of Bill and the other keepers lined up in front of a large stately looking house with braces of pheasant laid out before them. Victor wondered if the breeks Bill was wearing in the picture had just walked into the kitchen to put the kettle on. There were mole traps in great abundance, some in various states of disrepair. It turned out that the 21st century could not quite do without Bill's skill at mole catching and he was in big demand by the owners of the golf course, whose greens and fairways had recently fallen victim to the little pink shovels of the black velvet clad mammals. This supplemented Bill's pensions and gave him at least some connection with the land. After a lengthy discussion on the shoot, Victor finally managed to inform Bill of the purpose of his visit. Victor asked Bill if he had any alarm mines that he could borrow. These mines were used to warn of unwanted guests on a shoot, a blank shotgun cartridge being discharged via a trip wire. Victor had not really suffered the depredation of poachers during his time as Brockleston keeper and had not had the need to equip himself with such items in the past. Rather than tell old Bill too much, he made the excuse that he had lost a few birds in the last month and he thought that some lads from the village were visiting his pens in the night. He could have probably got Mowbray or the shoot captain to authorise the purchase of the mines, but that was a hand he did not wish to show them and he did not want to be seen buying them himself either. So a 20 mile trip to see Bill was the obvious solution. Bill took him out to the back of the flat. There was a small wooden shed next to the dust bins and Bill opened it up and peered inside. After some minutes of searching through ageing cardboard boxes and old tins, he came up with the goods. There were six mines wrapped up in oily rags, as good as the day Bill had collected them up on his last day as keeper. Victor smiled with delight; his journey had not been wasted. He drove back to Brockleston, arriving in the village by mid afternoon. He had a quick sandwich at the cottage and then spent some time at the kitchen table carefully removing the shot from several twelve bore cartridges. He then went out to the shed and made some short stout wooden pegs to secure some of the trip wires with. The plan was to place the mines in places around the shoot that would give him some warning of people approaching the pens. The unwanted visitors would have the same aim as the poacher but for different reasons he thought. He decided that the job was best done in daylight and he set off in the Discovery towards the village, intending to start at 'The Moss' and work his way across the shoot, making the final decision as to the exact placement of the mines as he went.

On his way past the pub he called in to see how Sarah was doing. He was met with a frosty reception when he entered the bar. Bill Stewart glared at him and greeted him in a strained formal manner. The place was empty apart from two draymen that were just finishing their pint after unloading some kegs. As the two men left Victor asked Bill where Sarah was.

"Well you might ask; I have sent her home, I can't have her in here looking like that. This place might be a bit out of the way but it's got a good reputation." Victor told Bill that he had not been happy at her going in to work as she was but this only made Bill more indignant. It was obvious that Bill thought the state of Sarah's face was down to the keeper's fists. Victor was on the edge of telling Bill what had happened but managed to stop himself, reason only just prevailing. Victor left the pub and turned his vehicle around, heading off to Sarah's house. When he arrived in the close one of Sarah's neighbours was out washing his car. Victor acknowledged him as he went up to her door, but he was ignored. The man turned away and continued about his task. It was nothing unusual for people in the close to behave that way; most had come there from nearby towns and did not speak to anyone that they did not know. But Victor believed it was probably more to do with the rumours that no doubt were now circulating in the village. Sarah let him into the house and told him that Bill Stewart had tried to get her to admit to him that Victor was responsible for the state of her face. She had decided to go back to her own place as she did not want to make things worse for him. Without being able to tell people what had really happened the case was proved in everyone's eyes locally. Victor had to agree but was loath to let her stay at the house alone. He knew that trying to convince her otherwise would do no good though. Before he left she did agree to stay in touch and let him know if anything else happened.

It was late afternoon when Victor got to the woods; the light was already fading and he would have to work quickly to get the mines in place before dark. He started at 'The Moss', placing a trip wire across the obvious clearing between the trees that led from the main ride to the pheasant pen, then securing the mine low on a tree trunk just behind a rhododendron bush. The wire was already difficult to see in the light and he thought he would have to be careful not to trigger it himself on his visits to the pen. He loaded the mine with one of his blank cartridges and moved on quickly. He wanted to place a wire across the small gap between the two parts of Jack's Slang as it was an obvious route for anyone crossing that way on foot, but decided against it as there were often cattle kept in that field. He decided to miss the drive out as there were no other good places, and carried on to The Long Gorse. There he placed mines on the hatches at either side of the wood. He varied his style of placement just in case his adversaries were quick learners. In Solomon's Wood he placed two mines fairly close together, their trip wires crossing the main path leading to the pen in the centre of the wood. The final mine was placed on the gate into Graves Spinney, the trip wire running across the top rail of the gate. The obvious way to enter the wood from the church side was by climbing the locked gate as tall blackthorns protected the wood on that side. He had managed to get the mines in place despite the final few being hard work as the light had gone. He did not bother with the drives on the other side of the Brockleston Road. He decided these were closer to his cottage and the village and hall and were at less risk than the outlying woods. His only concern was whether he would be able to hear the mines being triggered, especially those in Solomon's Wood and The Long Gorse, which were furthest away from the cottage as the crow flies. He was back at Keeper's Cottage by about 7pm. As he passed the door of the spare room he looked inside. Sarah's bag and belongings were still in the room. There were only the essentials for a night away but in some way it was good to see signs of another human being in the house even though it had been far too brief an occupation. He tried not to think too much about the situation and went outside to get wood for the fire. Just as he was putting the log basket down by the hearth the telephone rang. He rushed to answer it in the belief that it would be Sarah. It was Mowbray.

"I believe the afternoon went well too last Saturday; let's

hope this continues. Now there's just another matter that's come to my ears today that I want to ask you about." The agent went on to question Victor about the rumours in the village concerning him and Sarah. Victor told him about her being attacked in her house but for want of a better explanation said that it was her past associates demanding money. He wasn't going to have Mowbray believing it was him that had attacked her. "Well Drew, admirable behaviour, but you know what folks in the village are like; it's best not to get associated with such people if you know what I mean." Victor wanted to tell him to mind his own business but kept quiet; it was bad enough having Mowbray control his working hours let alone his private life. He thought it was out of character when Mowbray had rung to show his appreciation. Now he knew the real reason for the call. Mowbray rang off with his usual abrupt exit to conversation. The rest of the evening and night passed with little event. A patrol in the early hours revealed nothing unusual and none of the mines was heard to go off.

The following three days were much the same. Victor went about the business of checking hoppers and pens and carrying out his early hours' patrols. He almost managed to test out his mine in 'The Moss' on one of the nights, just stopping short of disturbing the trip wire as he felt it across his boot. He heard nothing from Sarah and he did not venture into the pub, not really wishing to engage in further conversation with Bill Stewart. He knew his absence around the village would only confirm to Bill and others that he had beaten Sarah up and was lying low; but he was starting not to care; he could feel himself sliding into the depression he had experienced after Susan's death. The thought of having to collect the food from the pub for the shoot on Saturday was just a detail to him. The shortage of sleep and the constant listening and watching, coupled with the solitude, were starting to take their toll. Talking to Labradors was all very well but the conversation tended to be a bit one-sided in the early hours.

# Chapter Five

THE 'LUCY-B' WAS AT ANCHOR just off Cat Island. The weekend regatta had gone well and most of the boat owners had stayed on to continue the socialising and make full use of the good weather. Life was uncomplicated when there was no itinerary, no deadlines to meet and nothing in particular to worry about. Johnnie Marchington had been aboard with Hugo and Jane for about three days. They had spent the time drinking, playing poker late into the night and lazing about in the sun to recover from excess. Johnnie by this time had started to tire of the place and was contemplating his next venture. He had broken up with his last girlfriend about a week before and had hoped to acquire a new one during the course of his little regatta. Unusually for him his desire had gone unfulfilled and this was really the root cause of his restless mood. Hugo was as always quite contented just being where he was with Jane. The three were having lunch on deck and making small talk about the previous weekend's events.

"Done any shooting Brocky?" said Marchington out of the blue, as he slowly ate King Crab washed down with cool lager.

"How do you mean old man?"

"You know, big game and the like."

"No, had a few days at Brockleston in the past; Father always insisted on it, not really my thing though Johnnie." There was a short silence. Marchington sat thinking; he had a very skilled way of looking across to study Jane's cleavage whilst appearing to be looking directly at Hugo sitting next to her. It did not fool Jane and she had started to grow tired of it over the last few days. In fact Johnnie Marchington had become a real source of annoyance, slapping her backside as the opportunity arose and generally being too familiar. She put it down to his lack of conquest at the regatta, but it was no less irritating for that. Jane rose from the table and made her excuses, going below deck out of the sun.

"Got talking to a chap on my boat on Saturday night, said he had been out to South Africa doing some big game shooting at some sort of ranch; sounded bloody good sport. Wouldn't mind a bash at that sometime Brocky, do you fancy coming along?"

"Why not Johnnie, a change of scenery might do us all good." Hugo as ever was quite prepared to just go with the flow. He had known Johnnie Marchington since their first year at Eton together and had been in some tight spots over the years with him, mainly all the doing of `Marchers`, as he called him most of the time. Marchington was away, South Africa and big game was obviously going to be the topic of conversation for some hours to come, so Hugo ushered him to the sun deck and asked for more drinks to be brought up to them. Jane could hear the excited conversation from below deck and decided to leave them to it. She tried to apply herself to reading a novel but could not help being drawn into listening to Marchington as he expounded on quotas of impala, blue wildebeest, zebra and other game. He had certainly been paying attention to the man he had been talking to previously. He seemed to have studied it in as much depth as he had the little valley between her breasts, she laughed to herself.

"What time is it in South Africa Brocky?"

"Haven't a clue, why?" Marchington got to his feet and strode off with a purpose. He went below deck to his cabin, retrieved some crumpled papers from his blazer pocket and picked up his mobile phone. He then spent the next hour or so making calls and talking dates and times.

The talk of shooting and the mention of Brockleston for once made Hugo think of the source of finance for his salubrious lifestyle. He picked up his own mobile, looked up Mowbray's number and pressed dial. He made three attempts before connecting and speaking to his agent. Mowbray gave a report of the previous Saturday's shoot and then went on to tell Hugo about his concerns regarding the gamekeeper's private life; the success story being played down and undermined by the character assassination that followed it. Mowbray had little to say about the rest of the estate's business and assured Hugo that all was well. He then started to outline his fears that the estate's income might be falling behind what could be expected of it and that it was advisable to start looking at ways to improve this by looking at alternative uses for land and buildings. Hugo realised that Mowbray was settling in for a long discussion and he was not really in the mood for it. He made the excuse that he was about to run out of charge on his phone battery and said he would discuss the matter at length in the future. He then cut Mowbray off and turned off his phone. As long as enough money kept flowing to support him Hugo was not too concerned about the exact amount and from where he was sitting the accounts of a grey, cold and damp English estate were not the most pressing matter.

"So how are things at home, if you still call it that?" Jane had returned to the deck, taking advantage of Marchington's absence and catching the tail end of the phone conversation as she approached.

"They sound alright I suppose; Mowbray's got some bee in his bonnet over Drew's private life, but it sounds like the man has the shoot running just fine so what the hell." Jane sat down next to Hugo and poured herself a drink.

"Well, sounds like you boys are off reducing Africa's wild life population; I thought all that had died out a long time ago."

"Yes, seems not though; might be a bit of fun. Are you coming along, Jane, if it comes off?"

"I don't know, I might just leave you two to get on with it for a while and visit my parents for a few weeks; I haven't seen them since last Easter." A quiet half hour passed before Johnnie Marchington re-appeared overloaded with enthusiasm for the proposed hunting trip. He then proceeded to go through it all with Hugo, trying to sort out the fine details.

* * * * *

Victor left the shade of 'Lady Jane's Moss' and set out across the field towards the road. He had spent the morning topping up hoppers and checking the pens. He had also walked up some of the outlying hedgerows to drive any straying birds back towards the woods. It was the day before the second shoot of the season and all was still going well. As he crossed the Brockleston Road and started out across the fields behind the 'Brockleston Arms' towards Home Farm he heard the distinctive sound of a shotgun cartridge going off. From the direction of the sound it was clear that the alarm mine across the gate at Graves Spinney had been triggered. He cursed himself for not having his vehicle with him; the quickest way to the wood was by road from where he was; going cross country would not reduce the distance by any amount. He had at least a mile and a half to cover on foot before he could even see the wood. He got back onto the road and set off towards the village, Storm lagging behind due to the fast walking pace Victor was setting. He made good time towards Church Lane but in his mind he felt as though he was crawling on his hands and knees and that he would never get there. He was prepared to try to flag down any passing vehicle but not one came his way. It was late Friday morning and usually there was something on the road. He felt he was making some progress as he turned into Church Lane from the Brockleston Road and headed towards the wood. Storm by this time was well behind; Victor was totally unaware of this, his mind being focused on getting to the wood as quickly as possible. From about half way down the lane Victor could make out the outline of the wood. He then noticed a car coming towards him. It was a small blue hatchback and it was accelerating as hard as it was able to, its worn suspension bouncing it around as it came into contact with the potholes on the edge of the road. The car made no attempt to slow as it approached him and he got into the hedge as far as he could to avoid being struck in the narrow lane. It passed, narrowly missing him, and carried on towards the village, its engine still protesting in pain through the noisy exhaust. Victor turned to watch the car, straining to read its registration mark but failing to get more than its prefix of `J` as it sped away. He also managed to see that there were two men in the car but would have been at a loss to have described them in any more detail than being aged around 30 with short hair. He then saw Storm ambling down the lane towards the car; he had been a good distance behind Victor due to the hurry and had not long since entered the lane by the look of it. The car continued at speed towards the dog, which was close to a small verge by now, one of the few wider areas of the lane. The old dog strayed onto the verge to give his hot feet a rest from the relentless hard road surface. Victor sighed with relief then gasped in horror as the car

47

suddenly cut into the nearside hitting the old dog. There was a loud bang and the sound of glass breaking. Storm flew sideways into the hedge and lay motionless. Victor ran towards the car which had now stopped on the road a few yards from the dog, his legs almost giving way with the shock, sadness and anger of what he had just witnessed. As he approached a figure got out of the passenger side and ran to the injured Labrador. It scoped up the limp body, opened the rear hatch of the car and threw the dog inside before getting back into his seat. The car then sped away just as Victor was getting close. Victor stood alone in the lane; there were tyre marks and broken glass on the verge, all that was now to be seen of the horror that had just happened in front of him. A flock of crows 'cawed' overhead like some mocking salute to the old dog in the silence of the lane. He could not really believe what had happened. One second his only thoughts had been on protecting the shoot, the next he was standing alone in a lane having just had his oldest friend deliberately run down and taken from him. It was some minutes before his mind started to actively think again. Perhaps they had not done it deliberately and whoever it was had not seen him either; they certainly did not make eye contact as they passed him. They may have picked up the dog to get it to a vet as quickly as possible. Something in Victor's baser instincts told him otherwise though and he had just been rushing to Graves Spinney after hearing an alarm mine go off. He was torn between heading on to the wood and going back home to call around the local vets. It took him several minutes to decide on checking the wood first; he than made his way to the spinney. Sure enough the trip wire across the gate had been pulled and the shotgun cartridge had been discharged. He hurried on towards the release pen, now starting to fear the worst. When he got to the pen his heart sank still further. The wire must have been tripped on their exit from the wood, because whoever had visited had clearly spent some time there and had not been put off by its sound. The pen had been destroyed, the tall wooden posts had all either been uprooted or smashed off at the bottom and the wire netting had been cut through and torn down. This would not have been so bad had it not been accompanied by the other horrors that decorated the scene. The birds that had not been scattered were dead and dying around the pen area. Pheasants were caught up in the tangled wire, some horribly injured and mutilated. There were injured birds flapping their wings and flopping around in uncontrolled reflex actions all over the area. Victor instinctively attended to all the injured birds, ending their torment as quickly and humanely as he could. The people who had visited Grave's Spinney were certainly not animal lovers. There was now no doubt in his mind that they were the same people who had just run over Storm in the lane and that the act was deliberate. The killing sprees of foxes in pheasant pens were nothing compared to what he was currently looking at. Charlie always made sure everything was dead and at least it was their natural instinct and could be understood. After completing his grim task, Victor sat down on the damp leafy floor of the wood, his head in his hands, sobbing like a child. Not since the initial shock of the news of Susan's death had he broken down in this way. The woods that were often his solace and escape from the outside world could provide no comfort. He felt as if his whole being had been torn open by hands callous beyond his comprehension. He started to panic at the thought of similar scenes all across the shoot. How many woods had they been in that morning after he had left them? He sprang to his feet and ran back to his cottage across the fields, his heart pounding at the unaccustomed pace, adrenalin from anger, fear and panic spurring him on. He picked up the Discovery and set out for the other woods. 'The Moss' was as he had left it just before hearing the mine go off. The pens in Old Jack's Slang and the Long Gorse were also intact. It was a different story in Solomon's Wood. Similar atrocities to those in Graves Spinney had taken place and this was one of the biggest woods on the shoot. Hatton and Hampton must have worked harder than they had done for years to cause the devastation. A considerable portion of the shoot's drives had been at least badly damaged for the season. As Victor set about the task of dealing with the injured birds he knew that he could no longer keep the situation from Mowbray.

After checking the woods and pits around Home Farm and Brockleston Hall, which at least were also undamaged so far, Victor steeled himself to meet Mowbray. It had got to 4pm and he wondered if Mowbray would still be around as he parked the Discovery in the estate yard which was between Home Farm and the hall. He found the office door unlocked and Mowbray was inside at his desk. Mrs Taylor the estate secretary had already left the office.

"Ah Drew, how's it going? You look worn out." Victor stood in the oak panelled office, steeling himself against emotion as he told Mowbray what had occurred that day. He failed to mention the original warning letter and previous occurrences; he did not want Mowbray to know he had been covering up.

"Good God, man, what the hell are we going to tell the shoot members? Those woods are now a dead loss, they will be wanting some of their money back now. We can't make up for the loss of those drives this season." Victor weathered the tirade from Mowbray and made no comment. There was nothing he could say and at least he knew he had tried his best. Apart from not having the ability to be in every wood 24 hours a day he had done everything he could do on his own to protect the shoot. He thought he could now at least openly ask Mowbray for some assistance from the other estate workers; however this conversation did not go well either. Mowbray's favourite subject of cost immediately came into the discussion and the loss of a good part of the season's game stock followed it close behind. Victor was on the back foot again and it was clear that there would be very little help from the agent. At least his previous decision to exclude him from what was going on still seemed justified.

"Have you contacted the police yet?" Victor told Mowbray that he had not.

"Well leave that to me, I will sort that out as it's estate business. You had better go and plan tomorrow's shoot; we will have to miss out those two woods and do the best we can. We haven't time to clear up the mess; and lets try to avoid anything else happening Drew." Victor left the office and headed back to the cottage. As he drove past Sarah's close he saw a white box van outside her house; two men were loading her furniture into it.

Victor entered the cottage and held the door open out of habit. He then realised that this was not needed anymore as Storm was not going to follow him inside. He sat down at the table and reached across for the telephone. He knew he was probably wasting his time but even so he rang all the local veterinary practices he could think of or could find in the local telephone directory. None had treated an injured Labrador that afternoon. The last glimmer of hope for his old friend died with the fading afternoon sun and the cottage was emptier than ever. He really did not want to get on with the business of working out the drives for the following day but what was left of the shoot was still to be run; so he applied himself to the task and got it out of the way. While he worked he could hear Mowbray telling Robbie Langdon what had happened and running him down to the captain. Just at the moment he hated the agent as much as the two unknown people that had devastated his life that day.

At around 8pm there was a knock at the cottage door and two police officers were standing outside when Victor opened it. One was a man in his late 40s whom Victor had seen around a few times over the years but never spoken to beyond a brief greeting; he had the relaxed air of a man who had spent a long time dealing with all types of people and situations. The other was in his early 20s, very smartly presented with an air of superiority that Victor took an immediate dislike to. Victor invited them into the kitchen and sat them down at the table. He was actually glad of the distraction from his misery. He made coffee for himself and the older officer, the younger having refused any. Victor told the tale of the day's events and the younger officer filled in several report forms. During the conversation it became obvious that the younger officer had very little interest in rural policing and even less understanding of the countryside. It was also clear that he disapproved of country sports. Victor could remember his father being on very good terms with the local policeman when there was one housed in the area. They had even gone out patrolling the woods together when there had been problems with local poachers. There was a lot that had changed in the last 30 years or more. With some people the gap between the town and the country was an enormous chasm that would never be crossed again. When the two left he was again alone in the cottage with his thoughts. It was going to be an even longer evening than usual. He knew that he would have to make another early hours' patrol of the woods and the likelihood of his enemies now being forewarned regarding alarm mines did not make him feel any better.

At 2am he set out to 'The Moss' and made his way across the fields, checking the drives. It was another clear night and the moon was up and bright. He checked as far as The Long Gorse before doubling back and checking the woods again on the way back to the road.

51

He saw no point in checking Solomon's Wood and Graves Spinney and moved straight onto The Hall Wood where he spent about an hour before quickly checking Home Farm and the duck pits. He could find no new damage and was back at the cottage for around 4.30am, where he retired for a restless few hours in his bed.

✳ ✳ ✳ ✳ ✳

On a dirt track at the rear of a disused plastics factory just outside Limcester a blue Ford Fiesta was being prepared for its final curtain. Elvis Hatton was pouring petrol from a green plastic can over the seats while Scott Hampton sat in the driver's seat of a green Renault Clio parked a short distance away with its engine running. Hatton threw the empty can on to the back seat of the Fiesta then stood back. He lit a ball of newspaper with his lighter and then threw the flaming paper through the open door of the car onto the passenger seat, stepping back as he did it. There was a loud whoosh as the unleaded fuel ignited, lighting the night with a bright yellow flash. Hatton ran to the waiting car and the two raced off through the old factory yard and onto the main road, only turning the car's lights on when they were safely away from the premises. The whole action was carried out with the practised ease of the professional, only the broad grins on their faces belying the pleasure they still took from it all. Just another old unregistered car burned out at the back of the derelict factory, nothing of great note to the police or anyone else locally. By the time the two had reached Brandley Park the inferno had died down, leaving nothing but a charred empty shell.

# *Chapter Six*

IT WAS A VERY DIFFERENT Victor Drew that drove out of the cottage gateway and headed towards Home Farm for the second shoot of the season that morning. The high spirits and anticipation of the previous Saturday now seemed unreal as the Discovery turned left just before the 'Brockleston Arms' and headed towards the shoot shed just before it. It was now a totally silent affair, there were no excited little whimpers coming from behind the dog guard for the first time in over ten years. Victor was not looking forward to the day, especially the first hour or so when all would have to be revealed to the guns and beaters who had not already heard what had happened. He arrived in the yard dreading his first conversation, no matter with whom. It turned out to be Robbie Langdon; Robbie had just got out of his vehicle as Victor arrived and stood waiting to speak to him when he saw him pull into the yard.

"How's things Vic? Mowbray rang me last night and told me what had gone on; it doesn't sound to me as if there's much you could have done to prevent it." Victor was at least slightly pleased to hear Robbie's words; the captain was a reasonable and realistic man and they had always got on well. He also knew what Mowbray was like and any respect he had for the man was only out of etiquette. They walked to the shoot shed together; Victor appreciated this support; making a lone entrance was something he had been dreading.

The usual group was assembled in the shed. The day's guests were all familiar to Victor as they had been to Brockleston may times before. Mowbray did not appear but this was not unusual. When Robbie called the group to order in the usual way he dispensed with the safety talk and went through the events of the previous day so that all present would know what had taken place and why the shoot would not be running to its usual form. As Mowbray was not present and Victor was not in the frame of mind to use them, the diagrams of the drives were dispensed with for the day. The morning would start as usual with the Brockleston Pits and then proceed to the drives in The Hall Wood. The duck drive went well again and nine brace of Mallard opened the bag for the day, with at least three quarters of the guns getting birds over them. As Victor was walking back to the yard at the end of the first drive Nick Jones came up alongside him. Nick was struggling to control his two Labs on their leads; it was the start of the day and they had not burned off any of their enthusiasm and energy

"Where's old Storm today?" Victor had to steel himself before he answered. He had not mentioned the dog to anyone so far as he could not bring himself to talk about it. He took Nick to one side and told him the tale, having to stop occasionally to pull himself together. The off duty policeman could see the distress Victor was in and was embarrassed that he had asked. A combination of police investigative skills and anger took over Nick and he could not help himself asking Victor too many questions about the detail of what had happened. He realised this and apologised.

"That's ok, I could do with your help on this one Nick; I'm not going to get any from Mowbray and I doubt the report I made to your colleagues last night will do much good the way you're short of manpower." Nick could not believe what had happened to Storm; he was as much part of the shoot as anyone to him and he appreciated that the old dog was not just a work tool to Victor. They were caught up by the rest of the party and the conversation was cut short. The group then set off for The Hall Wood, where Victor had managed to devise three good drives for the guns. The rest of the morning went well and by lunchtime 49 pheasants were added to the ducks on the game racks in the shed. Victor asked David Radford to collect the hot pot from the pub while he hung the game on the tracks, so avoiding another conversation with Bill Stewart. The conversation over lunch was mainly focussed on the sabotage and what organisation may have been responsible, but no good conclusions were forthcoming and it was all mere speculation.

Richard Mowbray looked the picture of affluence as he stood by the parade ring at Ludlow race course running his eye over the prospects for the 2.30pm handicap hurdle race. His sports jacket and flannels blended in nicely with all the other sartorial elegance around him. Mowbray and his wife had been asked to attend at the invitation of Sir Jack Melton who owned a good string of race horses including `Jack's Comet` that was running that day in the 2.30. Melton was the cousin of Richard Rotherby-Hyde and had really wanted to invite Lord Hugo and Jane to the meeting to get to know his Lordship a bit better; but had to make do with Mowbray in their absence or so the official story went. To his credit Mowbray did have more knowledge and enthusiasm for the racing world than he did for game shooting and his interest in the day's events was not all 'put on' for the benefit of Sir Jack. The prospect of a day out at the races and a free champagne lunch in influential company would have been a lot more enticing to him than a day in the mud of the Brockleston shoot even if he could have had a choice in the matter. Mowbray's wife Lydia was the perfect accessory for him in her new light tweed suit, fitting in well, making small talk with Sir Jack's wife Anne. Most of Sir Jack's fortune had come from shrewd investments in the property world. He was a ruthless individual when it came to making money from new developments and there were many areas of the countryside that had been changed completely as a result of his business acumen, including the redevelopment of the estate where Bill Flemming was once head keeper.

The afternoon's shooting activities commenced with a drive at Old Jack's Slang with the party then moving on to The Long Gorse. The two drives went well and Victor presumed this was partly due to some of the birds that had survived from the Solomon's Wood pen making their way across to these drives and taking shelter there. The day was concluded with a final drive at Lady Jane's Moss. There seemed to be very few birds in this wood but there were no obvious signs of any recent disturbances to the pen or any other areas; but something had happened there. The number of birds had never fallen off before Christmas in the past and it was only the start of the season. Victor was turning it all over in his mind as the horn blew to mark the end of the drive.

"Not so good in there today," remarked Robbie Langdon as he crouched under the barbed wire to exit the wood.

"No, it's really odd and I can't see the cause of it; something is up here too though, got to be," Victor's voice was no more than a harsh whisper, his comment was more the voicing of his own solitary thoughts  than a reply to Robbie. The day ended earlier than had been originally planned as there were only limited drives in the afternoon; Victor had made the full use of what was left but he could not extend the day further without the two desecrated woods. As the group made their way back towards Home Farm the keeper's thoughts were dominated by the events of the preceding few days. The day's bag of 86 pheasants and 19 duck was to do little to raise his spirits, despite this being a respectable total under the circumstances. The atmosphere in the shed was as jovial as usual; the rest of the party had not seen or felt the devastation first hand. There was much debate and banter as to whether the prize money for the sweep should be handed out or retained for the following week as nobody had guessed low enough to come even close to the total. Victor might have done if he had entered; the bag was a lot higher than he had dared hope for. In the end the money was finally handed over to Phillip Boddington, probably for fear of them never hearing the last of it had they not given him his prize. Victor could not recall ever feeling so miserable in the shed after a shoot; he had a flash back of the time he had sat there alone after the argument with Susan; at least then he had not been surrounded by cheerful conversation. Victor gave out the braces of birds and sat down next to Nick Jones. He was in no rush to leave, he didn't want to venture into the 'Brockleston Arms' and there was to be no company at all back at the cottage now. He was making inroads into a large bottle of whisky that was on the table in front of him. He was drinking the spirit neat; he usually had a splash of water in it, but he could not be bothered with that for the present. As the shed started to empty, the conversation got quieter and the words passed between Victor and Nick almost fell to the level of a conspiratorial whisper. It was not long before there were just the two of them left behind, the dropping temperature making their breath visible in the damp cold. Both had drunk more than they should have for driving home, but they were oblivious to the fact as Victor told Nick all about the events that had started with him receiving the anonymous threatening letter. Nick sat silently; his only actions were the occasional nod or shake of his head in disbelief and the pouring of more spirit into their glasses. Neither man had a brother of his own but the bond that existed between them in that cold shed at that moment was stronger than any blood tie. The anger and sadness swirling in the mist of their common intoxication was almost tangible as they shared their emotions and tried to make some sense of the situation. Nick knew that there must be some link with Sarah Stokes and wanted to speak with her to find out what she knew of her violent visitors; but this was academic for the time being as she had left the village. He also wondered how he would have got on in any case as he had met her professionally in the past during her wayward times and things had not gone well. He had spoken to her lately but it was only out of social politeness whilst on the shoot or in the 'Brockleston Arms'. He had not felt the confidence to engage in conversation for fear of her remembering him; although he did doubt that she would as her mind would have been clouded by the effects of hard drugs when they had met in the past.

"Do you want to go and have a look around now?"

"What?" asked Victor looking back at Nick with bleary eyes.

"Check the woods; it's an ideal time for them to do more damage, they will know that they have the place to themselves and there's no chance of you turning up."

"Blimey you're as much cop as country boy, Jones, aren't you? I wouldn't have thought of that one."

"I have spent too long amongst the scum Vic, I think like them now that's all." Victor checked his watch, well tried to at least; it was just after 8pm. The two cleared up the last of the glasses and Nick threw the now empty bottle in one of the rubbish bags by the door. They switched off the lights and locked up, Victor struggling to complete the operation due to his drunken state. Placing the key back on the ledge was no easy feat, but he got it there on the third attempt as Nick steadied him. They made their way to the vehicles and Nick let his dogs out to run around the yard; they had been in the back of his car for hours and were desperate to relieve themselves. He gave them both a drink and some dog biscuits before settling them back in. The sight of the dogs with Nick was a cruel reminder to Victor that there was no old friend in the back of his Discovery looking forward to some tea at the cottage. He felt the tears and anger welling up inside him. All the whisky in Scotland couldn't dull that pain.

"I need a walk to sober me up, can't bloody drive anywhere in this state can we? It had better be a long walk too Vic," Nick staggered back from the rear hatch of the car as he closed it.

The two set off towards The Hall Wood. They cast shadows across the ground as they walked out across the pasture land adjacent to Home Farm, the moon was up early and the darkness of the yard was soon left behind as they strode out across the grass. They walked in silence, the fresh air and stillness almost making their previous conversation seem foolish and strange. There was perhaps some small degree of embarrassment felt by them both as the fortifying effects of the alcohol started to subside. As they neared the wood they went into the shadow of the hedgerow; this was more a well-ingrained reflex than a conscious action. Long years in their trades had left indelible marks on their behaviour, marks that not even the good whisky could wash away. If there was anyone in the Hall Wood they would do well to notice the approach of the two men whose shadows now merged with those cast by the thorns. Inside the wood the silence hung like a thick black blanket, only interrupted by the occasional hoot of an owl or scream of a vixen. It was some minutes before their eyes grew accustomed to the darkness and they could set off along the edge of the ride to patrol the drives. Walking on the edge of the rides almost in the tree line was not easy; there were still plenty of briars reaching out onto the track like spiteful spoilt children tugging at anything within reach. The really hard frosts of winter had not come to lay them low yet and they had managed to make new growth since Victor had cut them back before the start of the season. Their progress was slow and tedious but they were both spurred on with the thought that there might be other visitors up ahead of them. There must have been very little of The Hall Wood that was not checked over in the end; they spent just over two hours walking in the shadows of the trees. The only things they saw were the wild life and the pheasants that had returned to roost. Nothing was said, but both men would

58

really have liked to have found somebody in the woods that night, someone to blame for the upheaval and deadly turmoil that had entered their lives. By the time they got back to the farmyard, the effects of a long hard day outdoors and the falling alcohol level had started to take their toll; they were exhausted and feeling the ill effects.

They sat in Victor's Discovery for a while, taking a rest and drinking up the last of the lukewarm coffee that remained in their flasks from the shoot day.

"Well I don't know about you Nick, but I'm all in, let's go and look at Lady Jane's Moss and than call it a night; we'll drive down there and leave the vehicles on the lane just short of the wood. I can't face walking across to the other woods and most of them are pretty worthless at the moment anyway." The two vehicles left the Home Farm yard and headed towards the village. There were a few cars in the car park at the pub, but otherwise the place was deserted; there weren't too many that ventured out to the 'Brockleston Arms' on a Saturday night at that time of the year. They stopped in the lane and switched off their lights, tucking the cars onto the narrow verge as far as they could. They cut through a small gap in the hedge and into the maize stubble field that surrounded the wood. There was no way of getting right next to the wood without offering a chance of being seen but they minimised this by keeping to the right hand hedgerow as far as they could before cutting across to the Brockleston end of the wood. The wood was strangely silent; there was not the slightest sound as they entered. Both men sensed this and felt it to be unnatural. Victor made his way to the edge of the ride with Nick following close behind, glancing around trying to make out any strange shape in the darkness. Victor suddenly crouched on his knees and pointed down the ride; Nick followed his action and peered over Victor's right shoulder, staring to see what the keeper was pointing at. As his eyes grew more accustomed to the darkness he could see a figure standing in the ride a couple of hundred yards away. The figure looked as if it was staring up the ride in their direction. They backed into the tree line to conceal themselves.

"Looks like you were right Nick, let's see if we can get closer and see if we can't introduce ourselves to this visitor." They made their way towards that part of the ride, staying back in the wood and making slow progress as they tried to negotiate the difficult undergrowth, fallen trees and low branches with as little noise as possible. Progress was painfully slow and Victor thought to himself that they had little chance of making ground on whoever it was up ahead of them. It was almost impossible to judge how far they had walked down the wood in the darkness and he felt the constant desire to get to the edge of the ride to see. After what seemed like hours, Victor stopped and signalled that they should go back towards the edge of the ride. The long clearing of the ride seemed to be illuminated compared to the darkness of the rest of the wood; the trees at its edge were like gaunt thin sentries silhouetted against the dim light as they approached. From this angle it was difficult to make out if there was anyone in the ride or not and Victor expected the shadowy figure to have been long gone in any case. He suddenly noticed a dark shape ahead to his left. He stopped in his tracks and stood staring. The figure was still there. He could make out what looked like a man in a hooded long coat, the hood drawn tightly around his face. The figure was still looking down the ride from where they had just walked. He clearly had not noticed their approach and Victor could not believe his luck at this. There did not seem to be anyone with the figure; Victor assumed that he must be a lookout; something else was going on in the wood somewhere. More than likely the pen was being attacked. Victor knew he must act quickly as time was short if he was to save the birds and the drive. He signalled to Nick to follow and they made their way further down the ride, keeping within the tree line. As they got behind the figure's line of sight, they made their way to the edge of the ride silently. Victor then tapped Nick on the shoulder and they burst from the tree line towards the figure. Nick instinctively overtook Victor and launched himself at the back of the figure; he reached forward, placing his arm across the front of its face, and swung his bodyweight to the left to bring the intruder under his control. To his surprise there was a loud snapping sound, the sound of splitting wood and the figure fell lifeless from his grip onto the peaty floor of the ride. The figure rolled over and two lifeless eyes stared back at them in the moonlight. They both stared silently at the figure; there was a piece of broken stake where its legs should have been and there were no arms in the coat sleeves. Victor took a small torch from his pocket and shone it at the strange scarecrow-like mass. The torch beam lit up something that was to haunt them both for a very long time. The battered and bloody face of Storm looked back at them from the hood. They stood in stunned silence; disbelief and horror combined to make the nightmare complete. A handwritten note in a dirty plastic bag was pinned to the front of the coat:

> You wouldn't listen would you my friend. What's it going to take to get you to stop?
>
> Your stupid tart has gone, your scabby old dog's dead.
>
> Give it up now or it's going to get worse, far worse than your simple half wit country mind can imagine.
>
> This is your last warning!

The old dog had once again returned to the woods but not through any desire of his own. He had been used to deliver a callous warning to his master in the very heart of the place that in life he had loved most of all. Victor dropped to his knees and went about the grim business of releasing Storm from the wooden frame that he had been tied to. He removed the hooded jacket from the dog and cast it to one side before leaving his old friend lying at the edge of the ride. The two men walked on down the ride without a word being spoken between them. They checked the rest of the wood and could find no further disturbance; there did not need to be, a harder blow could not have been struck on Victor. When they eventually got back to the road Nick broke the silence.

"Do you mind if I take these with me? You never know, they may be of some use." He indicated the jacket and the note that he had carried back across the field.

"Take them please, I don't really want to see them again. Thanks for being around Nick; it's been bad enough as it is." The two parted and drove on to their separate destinations, Nick back to his home and family, Victor to the empty cottage. The Brockleston Keeper was completely exhausted both physically and mentally; the past 24 hours had seemed like weeks and despite his mental state he collapsed into a deep sleep in the chair by the cooker within minutes of returning home.

It was mid morning when Victor awoke; the sound of the post dropping through the letter box onto the hallway floor raised him from the depths of his slumbers. As his eyes focussed on the clock the events of the previous day stole back into his consciousness. There were things to do and he had slept on into the day oblivious; he cursed himself and went about the business of preparing himself to leave the cottage. Collecting a spade from the shed he got into the Discovery and left for the woods. There in the light of a clear early winter's morning he dug a neat hole at the side of the ride in Lady Jane's Moss and said a last goodbye to one of the best friends he had known. If shooting continued at Brockleston at least the old lad would always be a part of it he thought to himself.

It is a strange phenomenon how thoughts and ideas that would be otherwise implausible enter the distressed human mind in times of extreme anguish and despair. It was at this time that such an idea came to Victor. He strode off towards the pheasant pen with the spade on his shoulder. Standing looking at the patch of fallen leaves in front of the gate to the pen he turned his idea over in his mind. Stark practicalities brought him to his senses and the difficulty in disposing of what would probably amount to around two tonnes of freshly dug soil discreetly and almost instantly brought him back to reality. He would have to think again. Disconsolately he left the wood and headed back to his Land Rover; apart from never sleeping again he had no idea how he was going to protect the shoot and provide sport to the end of the season. As he drove into the village he decided at least to clear up one little ambiguity that was hanging over his name. He pulled into the car park of the 'Brockleston Arms'. Bill Stewart was fussing around a table at which sat half a dozen nicely dressed folks out for a drive in the country and a Sunday pub lunch. As Victor stood at the unattended bar, he could see Bill was ignoring him, no doubt irritated at the sight of the scruffily dressed unshaven local lowering the tone of his pub at the week's busiest time. Victor waited patiently; he was in no hurry and there was nothing else in particular on his agenda for the day. The landlord eventually tore himself away from his valued customers and faced Victor across the bar.

"So what can I get you Mr Drew? Looks like you've been busy working this morning," Bill Stewart enquired with an unhidden tone of sarcasm in his voice.

"It's ok Bill, I thought I would just call in and clear something up with you whilst I was passing." Bill Stewart ushered Victor into the other side of the bar which was empty. He was apprehensive as to what was going to be said; he did not want to provide additional entertainment for his customers and lessen the pub's meagre trade any further.

"Well Bill, I have kept my mouth shut long enough about what's been going on around here and I know that you have thought the worst of me because of it..." Bill Stewart shuffled about nervously as Victor told him what had really happened to Sarah. Victor was just that little bit too loud for Bill's liking and he wished he had taken him into the living quarters. Victor was not holding back; he let Bill know exactly what he thought about the conclusions he had jumped to. This outspoken forceful man was something that Bill had not seen before and he could only listen in silence. Bill offered Victor a drink to try to calm the waters but this was declined; Victor was not in the mood for socialising. He left the discomfited landlord to attend to his now fascinated clientele and drove back to the cottage.

When the Discovery turned into the gateway of the cottage Victor saw that a Police Volvo V70 was parked to one side of the driveway. Nick Jones got out of the car as the keeper got out of the Land Rover.

"Hi Vic, thought I would stray out this way to see how you are doing." The two went inside and Victor sparked up the cooker after sitting Nick down at the kitchen table.

"I've just been and buried the old lad in the wood Nick; it all seems so final now, I never thought it would end this way; I always imagined him slipping away lying in front of this old cooker." The cop could think of no words to reply, pretty unusual for a man whose work partly consisted of breaking the worst possible news to the relatives of those slaughtered on the roads. Victor made some tea and produced some fruit cake.

"That car you saw, what was it?" Victor told the policeman about the blue Ford Fiesta. Nick in turn told him about the car that had by then been found burned out and that the two that had been sighted in it over the preceding weeks were also known to be past associates of Sarah Stokes.

"That explains quite a lot," commented Victor. It was the first time he had heard the names of Hampton and Hatton; whoever they were he already hated them. Nick had been busy that morning, arriving at work two hours early and searching every database available to him. He knew that a bit of rural crime would be no one's concern at Limcester Central so he had free range to take a look without standing on anyone's toes. The big question was why these two were doing this in Brockleston; this was something neither of them could understand. They were as far away from being concerned animal rights activists as it was possible to get and to go to all the effort they had to do gratuitous damage without obvious personal gain was even stranger. Being in the pay of an animal rights group was a possibility but highly unlikely if the group had got to hear about their killing spree. The evidence of their involvement did not even really amount to `circumstantial` but Nick was convinced they were responsible as at least the agents of destruction.

"I am going to see if they will fork out for 'ninhydrin`,[7] testing for fingerprints on that note that was left. They may have slipped up with that one; if the Force will bear the cost of sending it away we might be in luck." Nick knew that this was unlikely as the rural force kept a tight budget on forensic expenses and usually reserved it for `more serious` crimes. Nick was careful enough to keep some of the details back from Victor; he did not want him turning up at the Brandley Park Estate and exacting his revenge or worse still, and probably more likely, failing to do so and becoming a victim

---

7        A method of obtaining latent fingerprints from materials such as paper and cloth by using chemical (ninhydrin) treatment.

himself. He knew he had already divulged more information than he should have and that he was skating on the thin ice of the Data Protection Act if he hadn't in fact already fallen through it. Despite Nick being at the cottage for the best part of two hours neither could come up with any new way of dealing with the situation; so little progress had been made by the time the Volvo left Brockleston to attend a two vehicle injury collision on the outskirts of Limcester.

# *Chapter Seven*

T HE SOUTH AFRICAN AIRWAYS' INTERNAL flight from Cape Town touched down smoothly on the hot asphalt of Port Elizabeth Airport. It was 11am and the hot dry African heat hit the two Englishmen like a blast from an overheated hair dryer as they walked across the apron to the terminal building. Both were no strangers to warmth as they had spent many months in the Bahamas; but it was as if the thermostat had been given an extra playful tweak as they entered the Eastern Cape. It had been the last leg of their long and complicated journey from Nassau but Marchington was still acting like an over excited schoolboy on his first organised outing. He had been fortunate enough to have booked the excursion just in time. They had secured places in the very last week of the hunting season. Any later and they would have had to wait until the following March to hunt at the Verwond Voet Ranch. Jane Rotherby–Hyde had not travelled to South Africa with them but had shared the American Airlines' flight to Heathrow via Miami and had parted from them in England to visit her parents as previously planned. Once through the usual formalities of the airport they were met by Frans Van Hoek who was waiting for them as arranged with an air conditioned Mercedes minibus to transport them to the hunting ranch. Van Hoek was a larger than life character, a big man in all respects. He stood around 6'6" tall and must have weighed in the region of 20 stones. He had lived well on the fruits of the bountiful land that was South Africa. The plentiful supply of good wine and game had sustained him well over recent years, but he was still a hard looking man. His face could have been chiselled from the local rock and with very little care going into the process at that. The heavy set features and tanned weather worn face were punctuated by the pockmarks of long since forgotten teenage acne and the hairs on the back of his neck would not have looked too out of place on an English badger. He wore khaki shorts and his stout legs gave the appearance that the skin on them had rarely if ever been shielded from the African sun by any material other than the ubiquitous coarse hair that adorned them. Van Hoek shook their hands powerfully and directed the Xhosa native who was his driver and porter to stow the two travellers' baggage. He ushered them onto the minibus before taking his seat, sprawling out with an air of assured authority at the rear of the vehicle. "Mashihamba,"[8] he shouted at the Xhosa as the African climbed back into the driver's seat. The Mercedes moved off and headed out of the town, travelling north towards Kirkwood. The middle aged Afrikaner then started to tell them some background information as they drank cool beers from the on board cooler.

The Verwond Voet[9] Safari business was a family concern; it had been set up by Frans' Father and had taken its name from the day that Josef Van Hoek had viewed the land as a prospective buyer back in the late 1950s. Josef had tripped on some loose rocks and broken his foot whilst climbing a ridge to get a view across the plain. The two professional hunters were the third generation of Van Hoeks to inhabit the ranch. Frans' two sons Pieter and Johan were highly experienced guides and stalkers. They had practically grown up with a rifle in their hands under the watchful eyes of their father and grandfather. The hunting area extended to just over 150,000 acres which included land owned by the family and some which they had acquired shooting rights over. The vast area offered the full range of wildlife habitats that the Cape had to offer and despite the impetuosity of Johnnie Marchington he could probably not have selected a better place to try big game hunting.

Just under an hour later the Mercedes rolled through the gate in the boma[10] surrounding the Verwond Voet Safari Lodge. Two further Xhosa staff rushed out to meet the vehicle and the three Africans busied themselves taking the luggage to the guest rooms. Frans led Hugo and Johnnie to their rooms.

"We will have lunch at 1pm in the dining room across the yard; I will leave you two gentlemen to unpack and freshen up." The lodge was a modern looking affair consisting of a collection

8 Meaning "Let's Go!" in Xhosa (one of the Bantu languages spoken in South Africa especially by the Amaxhosa or Xhosa people of the Eastern Cape).

9 Translated as 'Wounded Foot' (Dutch/Afrikaans).

10 A rural fortress, protective fence/barrier or livestock pen in eastern and southern Africa.

67

of wooden structures built on the banks of the Kariega River. It seemed hopelessly out of place with the rugged landscape that surrounded it but it was a comfortable if not luxurious place and the security of the surrounding boma protected it from any unwelcome visits from errant wildlife. Lunch was a substantial meal, no doubt intended to welcome them to the country and get them into the frame of mind to enjoy the days ahead. It was the first time the two travellers had tasted anything so exotic as Roast Duiker[11]; the good wine that accompanied it, coupled with the effects of the beers imbibed on the journey up and the many hours of travelling, washed them into a state of relaxed tiredness as Frans expounded on the current locations of the game and his plans for the hunting the following day. They were joined at the table by Johan and Pieter who were unmistakably the two sons. They bore the stamp of Frans' distinctive DNA tempered by some of the elegant refinement of Anna their mother who sat at the far end of the table opposite her husband. Anna was a tall slim lady; still attractive for her years, who exuded an air of quiet authority as she instructed her house staff that were waiting on the table.

After the meal Hugo and Johnnie retired to their rooms for a rest during the main heat of the day. A late afternoon game drive to show them around some of the nearby hunting areas was planned for around 4pm. In the meantime they intended to at least partly recover from their journey and the more than adequate lunch.

***** 

Jane Rotherby-Hyde sat in the drawing room of her parents' house in South Kensington; she was thumbing idly through the pages of a society magazine, the sort of magazine that contained few words of any consequence apart from who had been at whatever social event in the last month and who had spoken to who etc. Amongst the many glossy advertisements for cosmetics, cars,

---

11    A medium sized antelope of sub-Saharan Africa (several different species/ subspecies exist).

clothes, property and the like, one stood out more than the others. Her old finishing school that had been in the grounds of a large stately home in the Midlands was featured; it was now a collection of luxury apartments and barn conversions that were up for long term leasehold. Melton Developments were the company that were offering up the properties for lease.

"I didn't know that Forrest Hurst College had closed; when did that happen?" she asked her mother who was writing a letter at the bureau.

"Oh at least a couple of years ago; I remember Uncle Jack meeting with your father over the insurance just after he bought it for development."

"So what happened? It shouldn't have closed; it must have been still popular, there was always a waiting list."

"Yes, we had your name down from the week you were born. But with all the recent scandal it could not have possibly kept going." Jane's curiosity was now aroused and the letter that was being written went on hold as she interrogated her mother. To summarise, there had been a string of occurrences at the girls' boarding school that had ruined an unblemished reputation going back some 40 years. These had culminated in the suicide of Miss Millicent Forrest, the school's founder and headmistress, after most of the girls were removed to other establishments and the once tireless flow of pupils had dried up to nothing. The school, like some others in the category, had its own stables and boarders were able to have their own horses and ponies with them. There had been several `accidents` with girls and their mounts getting injured, far more than is usual in equestrian circles generally. One unfortunate girl had been fatally injured when her horse had bolted across a main road and been struck by a lorry. Not surprisingly the hapless parents were not unforthcoming in their condemnation of Forrest Hurst. Jane sat in silence, turning over the memories of her time at the school, whilst her mother had gone to the kitchen to make some tea. Having the mental scrapbook of the happy days she had spent in her late adolescence in the company of Miss Forrest and her staff suddenly torn to pieces was a bitter and unexpected blow. She had already been regretting not going to the Eastern Cape with Hugo as within a few hours of being home she had grown bored and missed him terribly. Tolerating Johnnie Marchington now seemed a small price to pay. The discovery of the fate of her alma mater did nothing to lift her spirits.

"So what's old Hugo doing with himself now that you're over here Jane?" Richard Rotherby-Hyde asked his daughter as he entered the room with his usual jaunty air. There was no customary greeting from the underwriter to his daughter, just this direct question; even Jane thought this a bit odd despite growing up with her father's slightly irregular social skills.

"And how are you, too, Daddy seeing as I haven't seen you for months?" Jane retorted. The otherwise thick skinned Rotherby-Hyde felt slightly embarrassed by his daughter's rebuke and apologised, kissing her before sitting down and pouring himself some tea.

"Nice time at the club dear?"

"Yes, old Jack was down there; it appears that `Comet` won last Saturday at Ludlow and he's still celebrating. He told me he had asked you and Hugo along but you couldn't attend so he had Mowbray there instead." He then repeated his original question when he thought that he had redeemed himself socially. Jane told her father about the Africa trip.

"I hope they got some good insurance; it's a wild country and not just in terms of the animals they will be hunting."

"Do you ever think of anything else apart from business?" Jane was experiencing the usual irritation she felt in her father's company.

"Just being practical, that's all Jane dear." Mrs Rotherby-Hyde cleverly steered the conversation to calmer waters with the practised ease gained from many years of mediating between her husband and daughter. Penelope or Penny as she was known by all her family and friends was one of those people who never complained and made the best of any situation; this was probably the reason that her marriage to Richard had survived over the years. He was very single minded and was not an easy person to live with at times. The upside was of course the wealth that he managed to generate from his determined approach to business and almost psychic ability to predict financial trends. Both Penny and Jane were not so naïve as to not realise this and were grateful in their own ways.

"So what else did Jack have to talk about? Anything interesting? Jane has just seen the development at Forrest Hurst in here." Penny threw the magazine across to her husband.

"Oh just boring old business; he didn't mention Forrest Hurst, but that's a done deal now, he's just collecting on it."

"Done being the operative word by the sound of it when you hear all that's happened there," commented Jane. Her father did not respond; he collected the latest *Financial Times* from a small table by the door and left the room.

## ✳✳✳✳✳

The open-topped Land Rover left the confines of Verwond Voet Lodge heading along the dirt road towards the vast plain of the Karoo. The two Englishmen, now refreshed by their short rest, sat resplendent in hunting outfits freshly purchased from the Van Hoeks. There was something of the `theme park` about it all thought Hugo, but it bothered him little as he glanced at the excited expectant face of Marchington sitting beside him. His old friend had changed very little from their schooldays when it came down to it. The younger of the two brothers, Pieter, was driving and pointing out features. Frans and the other members of the family had remained behind at the lodge. The road got more uneven and dusty as they neared the plain. A group of Cape Springbok crossed the track just up ahead of them. Pieter stopped the vehicle to give them a chance to watch the animals and not hurry the herd along. They were a magnificent sight as they bounded past, the disturbed dust rising around and above them in the late afternoon air. The drive continued, giving the prospective hunters a taste of the area and sightings of several more species of game, some of which were at quite a distance and only visible through binoculars. Wildebeest, Impala, Kudu and Zebra were in plentiful supply as large herds of them made their way to and from waterholes. They even managed a fleeting glimpse of an elusive Cape Bushbuck which seemed to delight Pieter no end. Early evening saw the party back at the lodge and preparing for dinner which was to be a braaivleis[12] served out on the veranda overlooking the waterhole below. This would give them a further opportunity, while they drank sundowners as the meat was cooking, to observe game.

12      A traditional South African Barbecue.

Nicholas Gordon

A family of Warthog tentatively approached the waterhole amongst a herd of Zebra just as Hugo and Johnnie arrived on the veranda. It was a surreal scene as they drank the first gin and tonics of the evening and chatted to two German hunters who were about to depart the following day. The two Germans had nothing but praise for their hosts of the last eight days and were sad to be leaving. They were joined by Pieter and Johan shortly afterwards. The two Van Hoek brothers outlined the plans for their first hunt on the following morning. It was to be an early start and they would be heading off as two separate parties, Hugo with Pieter and Johnnie with Johan. This was how it was always done with each guest always having the exclusive services of his own professional hunter.

Just after sunrise the following morning two Land Rovers left the lodge and headed off on an early morning hunt. Hugo and Pieter headed off to an area of veldt some distance away with the main intention of stalking Black Wildebeest whereas Johnnie's intended quarry was the Cape Springbok on the Karoo. Hugo looked down with some trepidation at the Winchester Model 70 rifle that he was cradling. It was a very long time since he had handled anything other than a shotgun and even then it had been a comparatively much smaller .22 BSA rifle, shooting at rabbits from the front terrace of 'Brockleston Hall' with his late father.

"Don't worry Sir, many folks who come here have not even held a firearm before; you're in good hands, trust me," Pieter remarked, sensing Hugo's mood with uncanny accuracy.

"Believe me, I prefer it that way; over-confident folks make me nervous. They aren't easy to control in the heat of the stalk," he added, smiling. There was something reassuring in the confident, broad South African accent with which he spoke. A short time later Pieter halted the vehicle by a small clump of acacia trees and stood looking out over the veldt with his binoculars. He had spotted a herd of Wildebeest grazing about a mile and a half away to the northwest. Approaching the herd directly would have blown the scent of the men directly down wind to the herd and despite there being reasonable cover with small trees and scrub on the approach the animals would have sensed their presence long before they had got within range. Pieter's plan was to approach in a wide arc, circling to the west away from the herd and coming around to the north of them on some slightly higher ground with cover from a slight ridge. Pieter set off ahead with Hugo just behind with the weapon slung across his shoulder. The professional hunter stole across the terrain with silent speed, travelling as quickly as he thought Hugo was capable of doing. The herd could move off at any point if they were alarmed by the slightest thing and they would then be hard to reach on foot, especially if they crossed down wind of the hunters. As they stole across the veldt, making use of any scrap of cover they could find, the heat of the day was increasing all the time and Hugo began to feel the effects of the pace early on. He kept up with Pieter despite this, determined to hold his corner and compete with anything that Marchington was to achieve. They may have been good friends but schoolboy competitiveness still thrived between them many years after they had departed the playing fields of Eton. They stalked on, slowly circling the herd at a safe distance, Pieter stopping periodically to check on the position of the animals with the binoculars, making sure they had not taken off. When they eventually came to the north of the herd and started to move closer to them across the raised ground Hugo was relieved as the pace of the stalk slowed and Pieter moved slowly and more stealthily from cover to cover. One of the old bulls turned and looked in their direction, testing the air as if he sensed they were there. Pieter froze in his tracks with Hugo doing the same a split second later. They waited for what seemed hours before the animal settled back to grazing and they could again start to close in. When they were just short of the apex of the slight ridge Pieter went down in a prone position and started to scan the herd with his binoculars. He turned to Hugo and spoke in an almost inaudible whisper, "That old bull is a trophy animal if you want to try for him; he will not be cheap but if you want a good example he's the one or we could just go for a culling animal, it's up to you?" Hugo deliberated; he knew the decision must be made in seconds, all the effort and luck of the stalk dictated as such.

"Ok, trophy it is." Hugo passed Pieter the rifle and the hunter took a look at the quarry through the scope before signalling Hugo to crawl forward and take the gun. Hugo shouldered the weapon and took his first look at the bull.

"Ok, it's a good angle and just short of 175 yards; you need to hit him two thirds of the way down the shoulder facing us if you can." Pieter handed Hugo the ammunition and he loaded it into the breech of the Winchester via its bolt action with what looked like practised efficiency despite his nerves. Pieter nodded his approval as Hugo took aim at the 'clown of the veldt'. The old bull looked up to face Hugo as Lord Brockleston's finger tightened on the trigger. A tiny fraction of a second later the deadly slug made its journey through the hot African air, entering the Wildebeest via the approved spot on the shoulder and passing through the great heart. There was a loud deep bellow from the beast, his back arched and his hind legs kicked out for the last time as he fell to the dusty ground, accompanied by the crack of the rifle's report and the thundering hooves of the rest of the herd as they stampeded away.

"Well done Sir, you will not get better than that anywhere." They made their way across the coarse grass to where the animal lay. Already flies had started to gather on the freshly spilled blood as Pieter struggled to arrange the beast into a position where it looked as if it had just lain down to take a rest. He propped up its head with two short sticks he had been carrying for this purpose. Hugo watched the procedure, regarding it as a slightly macabre rite before taking up his position kneeling next to the animal with the Winchester in his hand for the customary photograph. About 20 minutes later Frans Van Hoek arrived with a party of three native workers in a small rough terrain lorry and the beast was hauled onto the back with the aid of a small crane mounted on the vehicle. All the dignity of the once magnificent beast was instantly lost with the sight of the modern machinery. It may as well have been just a piece of casualty livestock being collected by the local hunt kennels from a farm in an English shire county. Hugo and Pieter rode back to where they had abandoned their own vehicle on the lorry. It was a miserable journey thought Hugo, far removed from the stalk where they had competed on foot with the natural protective instincts of the animal. The rest of the party did not appear to share any of his negative thoughts; there were broad grins all around. A satisfaction in providing the end result of hard work and years of experience to a paying guest.

Back at Verwond Voet the 150 kilo animal was unloaded to a building that was fitted out for the purposes of skinning and butchery. Frans expertly measured the dimensions of the head and horns which would be passed onto whoever was charged with eventually mounting the trophy back in England. The process of preparing the trophy was then commenced by the skinners. Hugo then went off to his room to shower and change for lunch. It was some time before Johnnie Marchington arrived back at the lodge. His morning had not gone so well. They had located and stalked a group of Springbok for several hours without success; the wind had kept changing and alerting the group to the presence of the hunters and the quarry had finally charged off across the plain. The party had not even got close to a position where a shot could be taken. Johnnie's morning was then made even worse by the news of Hugo's success, despite his friend's reticence in making much of the affair.

"What will you do with it?" Johnnie asked as they sauntered towards their lunch.

"I expect I'll have it sent to Rowland Ward of Piccadilly; it's the only option really, and all the old trophies at Brockleston have been mounted by them, that I do know. They have been going since 1892."

"I wish my family's history was as impressive as yours Hugo; you make me feel like a right upstart at times like this."

"Come on old man, it's not where you are from but who you are that matters; let's get into Mrs Van Hoek's cuisine again, I'm famished." Despite Hugo's last comment the situation did kindle some unexpected thoughts as lunch progressed. Thoughts of walking down the long gallery at the hall as a boy, marvelling at the trophies collected by his ancestors from a time when Europeans were just discovering Africa as a hunting ground. These trophies were from Kenya and Uganda; he knew as he had studied them avidly at the time. He could still see the inscriptions on the little brass plaques that were placed below them. He had never had the fascination with hunting that his grandfather had but he did feel the excitement and longing for new and strange lands that must have partly driven the early adventurers. He was beginning to understand the almost eccentric affection that some Englishmen had for the distant vast continent. He now wanted to see a lot more of it and experience what remained of its true nature before the advance of commercialisation destroyed it forever. The trip he was on with Marchington struck him as a prime example of its exploitation, even though this was a comparatively minor operation in the grand scale of things and it was a decent enough family trying to make a living and preserve its past colonial lifestyle. He was suddenly aware that he had been distant and uncommunicative at the table; he hoped that this had not been noticed as he had momentarily lost track of time. He joined in with Johnnie's enthusiastic conversation with the Van Hoek brothers, covering up his hopefully unobserved lapse in social skills. Marchers had regained his enthusiasm as he had been reassured by Johan's calm optimism and was again his old self, asking questions and making plans as he enjoyed Anna Van Hoek's excellent Duiker pie.

# Chapter Eight

"**I**KNOW YOU FEEL STRONGLY about these things, PC Jones, but this is a bloody dog we are talking about, nothing more than a fail to stop animal accident when it comes down to it. Have you any idea how small my forensic budget is? I can hardly cope with the submissions for serious crime; my department are being held back with their enquiries as it is." Detective Chief Inspector Bob Lewis sat back in his chair in the tiny office overlooking Limcester town centre. He wasn't an unreasonable man, but the constraints he had been put under by a lack of proper funding had hit hard and made him very protective over finances due to pressure from above. Nick thanked the senior detective for his time and went back downstairs to the traffic office. The result of his enquiry had been expected but it was still just as frustrating when his suspicions were confirmed. His argument that it was linked to Hampton and Hatton had not cut any ice. He had hoped it would have as the two were on the list of target persistent offenders for the division. He should have made a start on a pile of accident files which were lying in his tray whilst it was a quieter shift but he could not be bothered despite some of them now getting a bit close to their target dates. Routine enquiries appealed even less than they usually did. He collected his patrol equipment and went to the board in the office where the vehicle keys hung. He picked up the keys for an unmarked Vauxhall Vectra and made his way out to the back yard where the patrol vehicles were parked.

The wet November Tuesday afternoon just about summed up Brandley Park as the silver Vectra entered the estate. Nick had no particular plan, he was just patrolling. He was out on the roads of the division ready to respond to any calls and looking out for anything of interest. He would have no problems justifying his presence on the estate to anyone if called to do so. He had never got completely used to the way some of the people lived there. He shook his head in silence as he saw a group of youths hanging around the front of a tired and abused looking corner shop. They were no doubt waiting to cause a problem for some poor unfortunate who happened to come by; such was the extent of their imagination when it came to providing amusement for themselves. He had long since given up trying to have constructive conversations with these people and pitied the poor community officers whose job it was to do so. Litter and graffiti were everywhere; there was no surprise that the same people who were responsible for this thought nothing of throwing the rubbish from their cars into the lanes of Brockleston and similar places when they passed through. It was just the normal way of behaving to them. A green Renault Clio passed the police car, heading in the opposite direction. Nick recognised the distinctive features of Hatton in the driver's seat as it went by. There was a figure in the front passenger seat; no doubt it was Hampton. There was a brief eye contact between the two men and Nick knew that Elvis had noted his uniform. An unmarked traffic car might have gone unnoticed by otherwise respectable motorists but to this firm it might as well have had a fluorescent constabulary crest on it. The Renault's driver speeded up out of pure instinct. Nick knew that there was very little point in trying to turn and follow. He knew from bitter experience that there wasn't a trick that the two didn't know and they were like rats escaping in the familiar surroundings of their own stinking sewer. Nick pressed on into the estate, partly to make them believe he had not noticed them, but mainly in response to the idea he had just had. He pulled over after the Renault had gone out of sight and dragged a blue fleece top out of the bag he carried in the passenger foot well. He put the fleece on, discarding his fluorescent jacket and folding it up so that only its plain black lining was visible on the back seat. He neatly stowed his white-topped traffic patrol cap underneath it. This was a token gesture he knew; most of the residents of the estate were equally as wise as the two that had just made off. He made his way towards Hampton and Hatton's flat, turning off both his personal radio and the vehicles main set as he went. He parked the Vectra just behind the block; and as casually as he could, walked in through the entrance and up the flight of malodorous stairs to the door of their flat. The stairwell was deserted as usual and luck was on his side for once. When he pushed at the door it opened, they had not bothered to secure it. Repressing the urge to vomit at the smell that met him as the door opened, he entered the hole in which the two slept. Hanging on a hook just inside the door was a jacket that matched the one that had formed poor old Storm's shroud and lying discarded on the hall floor was a canvas bag that contained some cord and two small hand axes. The bag smelled of the woods and the cord looked like that used to tie the dog to the makeshift gibbet. There was no doubt in the officer's mind who had been visiting Brockleston. He searched the rest of the flat looking for anything else of significance, but apart from unimaginable filth and the odd block of cannabis resin there was nothing else of interest. He left the flat as he had found it, hoping that his visit had been unobserved. On turning the situation over in his mind there was little in the form of strong evidence and also his entry into the flat had been illegal in any case. But at least he had confirmed something in his own mind. He could not remember ever feeling so angry towards criminals, he had always hated most of them but this time they had entered his own personal world and were destroying it. The one place that he used to be able to escape from the realities of his working life in the shadows of urban depravity had been entered by those very demons that he wished to avoid. Even more frustrating was that his own organisation could not be bothered to help him despite his years of service to it. Victor Drew and himself appeared to be all that stood between Brockleston Shoot and its demise.

\*\*\*\*\*

Victor walked into the Brockleston estate office and asked if Mowbray was available. The secretary, Mrs Taylor, went into the rear office and returned, asking him to go through. The agent welcomed him and asked him to take a seat. Victor sat in the chair opposite Mowbray's old oak desk; it was like some scene from a television costume drama with a peasant coming to beg for leniency from an overbearing landlord regarding the overdue rent. Victor asked Mowbray if he could purchase some extra feed hoppers to start feeding the birds again in the woods that had been attacked, in an attempt to hold the game on these drives. Mowbray sat silently for a few minutes before reaching behind him for a ledger. He placed the account book down on the desk and opened it, flicking through the pages before running his finger down a column of figures.

"Well I suppose we can stretch to a few pounds, but there's not much left in the budget for this season." It was a slightly more hopeful but not too dissimilar scene to that which had occurred at Limcester Police Station earlier on that afternoon. The agent said that he would consult with the shoot captain over the matter of getting some more money out of the members before he would make a final commitment. Victor asked if he could do this sooner rather than later as time was short if they were to avoid the birds straying too far.

"I'll let you know as soon as I can; I suggest you get on with straightening up the mess in the meantime. Take a tractor and trailer from Home Farm and get all the debris away to the old tip." Victor left the estate office; he had experienced worse results with Mowbray so all was not yet lost.

As it was not too late in the afternoon Victor decided to make a start on clearing up the woods and drove the short distance to Home Farm where he collected a tractor and trailer and borrowed a few tools to avoid having to stop off at the cottage. It was still raining fairly hard as he drove along Church Lane towards Graves Spinney. He could hardly see through the tractor's windscreen as the perished rubber of its wiper blade made a token effort to clear the glass. He entered the wood through the gate near the church and picked his way down the narrow ride to the remains of the pen, the branches on either side brushing down the sides of the tractor and trailer. He set about the business of clearing up the broken wood and wire. There was now little evidence of the slaughtered pheasants. Foxes and other scavengers had made use of the sudden bounty and only a few feathers and the odd bone remained. He busied himself breaking up what was left of the pen and loading it onto the trailer. One of the old original posts of the pen refused to move; it was broken about a third of the way up and he could not get enough purchase on it to remove it from the ground. It was a post that had always been there in his recollection; he could not even recall his father putting it there. He unhitched the trailer and reversed the tractor up to the post. After tying a short length of rope between the base of the post and the tractor's hydraulic arms he used the system to raise the stump of the post from the ground and drove a few yards to remove it from the earth. The post gave little resistance to the machinery and it was soon tossed onto the trailer. As Victor walked back towards where the post had been the carpet of leaves suddenly collapsed and there was a dull earthy thud as an area of ground about two yards across fell into the earth, exposing a hole about seven feet deep. He stepped back in surprise, considering himself lucky that he had not gone into this chasm himself with about three tonnes of tractor on top of him. He shuddered at the thought. He tentatively approached the edge of the hole; the rain was now forming muddy pools in its depths and small rivulets of soil mixed with rainwater were running down the sides. The hole was too deep to venture into without fear of not getting out again unaided. He slowly walked around its sides, wary of further collapses, and tested to see if the earth around it was solid enough to support his weight. The ground held firm, in total contrast to the sudden movement he had witnessed only minutes earlier. Curiosity getting the better of him, Victor found a longer length of rope in the trailer and tied one end to the tractor's hitch bar and then roughly measured enough length to reach the bottom of the hole before tying this end around his own waist. As the gamekeeper lowered himself over the edge of the newly formed pit a sweet earthy smell met him. It was neither pleasant nor unpleasant but strangely familiar although he could not think where from. He half slid, half fell down the unstable side of the hole, landing awkwardly on the soft damp soil at the bottom. At least it was firm enough and he had not continued through its surface to some new depth. He had not realised how much the light had faded and the pit now seemed dark and gloomy as he looked back up the rope to his promise of security. The earth beneath him was barely visible as he felt around with his fingertips in the gloom. He felt something hard beneath his hand and brushed the surface away, exposing something that was lighter coloured than its surroundings. He reached down to pick it up with both hands and felt some resistance. He tugged at the object which then suddenly released with a cracking sound like that of a small dry branch breaking in the wind. He recoiled in shock as he brought the object up from the darkness and his brain registered what it was. It was the bones of a human forearm; the radius and ulna were clearly visible and the jangling bones of the hand followed at the end furthest from him, like some macabre rattling costume jewellery, the dried sinews still keeping the old bones together despite their centuries underground. He threw the nightmare back into the darkness and scrambled back up the rope in his blind panic, his feet bringing down showers of earth from the sides of the pit as he ascended, imagining every lighter patch of earth to be a skull staring back at him outraged at his audacious intrusion into its lost world of silence. He crawled out and away from the edge of the hole, almost expecting something to reach out from it and haul him back in. As he stood desperately trying to undo the rope from his waist the familiar surroundings of the wood started to calm his nerves and he laughed to himself quietly. So the old tales were true, he thought to himself. He collected up the last remaining bits of debris and hitched the trailer up. It was by now completely dark and the tractor's lights left a lot to be desired; there was just one dull headlamp working and the trailer had no lights at all. He decided to drive across the fields to the cottage instead of risking it on the roads. The tractor and trailer could stay behind the cottage for the night. As he travelled across the dark landscape with only the drone of the old diesel engine and the sound of the rain for company his thoughts returned to his ongoing problems. The strange occurrence he had just endured might be of some use to him if he was to exploit it properly, he thought.

The following morning Victor was up at 4am. He was in the shed pulling out a roll of old carpet that had lain in there since the day he had moved into the cottage with Susan. He loaded this onto the trailer along with some wooden joists and lathes that were also lying in the shed, before driving back across the fields to the spinney. He returned to the hole that had appeared and worked there frenziedly for over two hours. By the time he had finished there was a wooden framework around the edges of the pit with thin lathes stretching across it. He threw the old carpet across the hole, cut it to size and secured its edges loosely to the framework. He then covered the structure with a layer of soil topped with fallen leaves to match the surroundings. Before 8am he was at the old tip at the back of the Home Farm getting rid of the load from the trailer. He stopped off at the cottage for some breakfast before going on to Solomon's Wood to clear the ruined pen there. It was lunchtime before he returned the tractor to Home Farm and picked up the Land Rover. In the afternoon he returned to the woods and topped up the hoppers. He put out extra lines of food in Solomon's Wood to try to hold the birds and also collected an alarm mine before going on to Graves Spinney. At the spinney he set up the mine with the trip wire running across the pit just underneath the carpet. He replaced the soil and leaves he had disturbed and then he realised there was nothing really to lure anyone to the trap; the pen had been the focus of their attack and it was now gone. His spirits sank. How could he have been so stupid he thought. All he had now was something that he had to keep innocent folks away from and some wasted hours of time that could have possibly been used more productively elsewhere. As he drove back down Church Lane towards the village he turned over the problem but could come to no sensible conclusions. He decided that he had done enough for the day and headed back to Keeper's Cottage. Why couldn't the fortuitous hole have appeared by one of the pens that was still intact, but there again they weren't in Graves Spinney with its long forgotten past and perhaps plague pits that had long since given up the flesh of the bodies deposited there, leaving the ground open to the ingress of hundred of years of rain water to wash away the soil beneath.

Victor had been at home for a couple of hours making a token effort at domestic work in the cottage when the telephone rang. It was Robbie Langdon. The shoot members had got together and come up with the money for half a dozen extra pheasant feeders. Robbie was his usual hopeful self and this combined with the encouraging news over the feeders raised Victor's spirits slightly. He was to go and pick up the feeders from the suppliers the following morning and get them out into Solomon's Wood and Graves Spinney as soon as he could, in the hope of getting some birds back for the following Saturday's shoot. There was no mention of any contribution of estate funds towards the feeders and no doubt this had not even been suggested by Mowbray but at least he had contacted Robbie and set the wheels in motion so Victor decided not to think too badly of him this time. The end result had been satisfactory and there was now at least a good chance of holding some pheasants in the damaged woods for the time being. By 10.30pm the last logs from the basket had been burned and Victor went outside to fill it with fresh wood before going to bed. He stood in the yard and listened for a few minutes as he was returning to the cottage. He was hoping to hear the sound of an alarm mine from the spinney, but there was nothing apart from the wind in the trees and the distant sound of a car on the Limcester Road to disturb the silence. He picked up the basket and carried it inside. He fed the old cooker with a couple of logs and closed it down for the night before going upstairs. He opened his bedroom window a couple of inches in the hope of making any sound from the woods that bit more audible; the cold of the night was a small price to pay he thought as he put extra blankets across the bed.

Victor woke around 6.30am. If there had been any trip wires pulled in Graves Spinney he had not been lucky enough to hear them. He set out to check for himself about half an hour later but found everything as he had left it; well almost, a fox had been digging at one of the edges and he had to make some running repairs to the covering of soil and leaves, but apart from that all was as before. After a very quick tour of the other woods and some breakfast he set off to collect the new feeders. His plan was to have them installed in the woods and filled with grain by the end of the day. The suppliers were located about three miles from where Bill Flemming lived and he was toying with the idea of calling in on old Bill as he was passing. In the end he decided not to; he would not have been able to make it a short visit without being impolite as he knew how old Bill liked company and he certainly had a lot to tell the old keeper. As it was it was early afternoon by the time he returned to Brockleston and got to Solomon's Wood. He placed four of the feeders about 30 yards apart in a line passing through where the pen had been and filled them up with a mixture of wheat and pheasant pellets. He then set off to Graves Spinney to do similarly with the two remaining feeders. He placed the feeders either side of the covered pit, the thought that the feeders or their customers might at some point be the target of further sabotage striking him as a distinct possibility. They would possibly provide the bait that he so desperately needed.

Over the following days and nights Victor waited and listened for the sound of the alarm mines; he deliberately avoided straying too far out of earshot of Graves Spinney whilst avoiding actually going near the wood itself. He kept his work activities in that area of the shoot to a minimum. He did all he could to encourage the intruders to visit the spinney but by Friday afternoon nothing had happened. He checked the wood at 1am on Saturday as he made his patrol to make sure all was well for the day's shoot; and apart from further attention to the edges of the pit by Charlie Fox nothing had moved. He was relieved to see that the levels in the hoppers had gone down and it looked as if a reasonable number of birds were feeding there again. He perhaps listened even more intently for the alarm mines during the few hours he spent in bed after this last patrol before another shoot day.

# *Chapter Nine*

THE SHOOT SHED LOOKED MUCH the same as usual as Victor examined Mowbray's map of Graves Spinney. He had arrived at Home Farm a little earlier than usual to plan the day's drives and to decide on his plans for keeping the beaters away from the area of what had been the release pen in the spinney. The early morning light streamed through the dirty windows onto the trestle table, showing up the powdery white dust from the grain that was stored in the loft above; the paper diagrams raised small clouds of the stuff as Victor shuffled them around as he mulled over the order of the drives. He was going to bring all the woods back into play. His intention was to show that the shoot was back to full business and running as it should be. By the time the first guns and beaters started to arrive he had organised the day and decided on a plan of action.

"Morning Vic, how did you go on with the new feeders?" Robbie Langdon was the first to arrive along with his guest for the day.

"Oh, fine thanks, I've got them in place and by the look of it the birds are holding well again. We need to be careful in Graves Spinney though; they're a bit wary there, so I've got some extra instructions for that drive."

"Right, just let them all know. I'll make sure they stick to them." Robbie escorted his guest to the table opposite and they were soon joined by David Radford who opened up his little book and started taking the numbers and money for the usual wager on the bag. Within a few minutes the shed was full; there were rarely any latecomers at Brockleston on shoot days. It was the highlight of the week for most if not all of them. Mowbray did not arrive and when Victor asked David Radford about him he said that the agent had been invited to another race meeting by Sir Jack Melton.

"He keeps his fingers in a few pies, does Mowbray,"

commented Victor. David Radford then started to laugh; Victor looked at the farmer, bemused. "Pies, Melton Mowbray, nice one Vic."

"Ah, pork pies." Victor smiled back, not really in the mood for humour but not wishing to appear miserable. There was one other person missing that Victor had been expecting to arrive. Nick Jones had not appeared and this was a rare occurrence; there were very few shoots that he did not manage to attend. The customary procedure was followed and the day's activities were outlined to the party. Victor spent more time than usual going through the procedure for Graves Spinney. He was to be in the beating line on a path that would pass through the centre of where the pen had been and he would be directing the beaters either side of him to move outwards, away from him, giving the area a wide berth in the supposition of not causing too much disturbance to birds that had returned to that part of the wood. Mowbray's plan of the wood was excellent for this purpose and some additions to it by Victor that morning made it complete. It was a plan that was not to be tested that morning, it turned out.

"Hey, what the hell do you think you are doing?" There was a sudden shout heard from outside the shed. It was muffled by the thick old wall as it had come from where the vehicles were parked and there were no windows on that side. Phillip Baddington rushed back into the shed; he was breathing heavily and his face was flushed red.

"Some buggers have been slashing all the tyres, I've just disturbed them." The party left the shed and hurried to the vehicles; most of them were now sitting on flat tyres which had ragged slashes in their walls.

"I saw one run off back into the lane, then a car made off towards Brockleston. I couldn't see the car as it was behind the hedge and he had his back to me so I didn't get a look at him either, he had a red coat on though." Phillip struggled to part with information as he breathed heavily. Robbie Langdon's pickup was still intact and he got into it and screamed out of the yard heading off towards the village. The rest of the party cursed and inspected their vehicles, most of which had been damaged. It was clear that the four wheel drives had been specifically targeted to prevent the shoot having transport across the fields. The ordinary cars had not been touched. Apart from Robbie Langdon's pickup there wasn't one off road vehicle intact; they all had at least two punctured tyres and were prevented from moving. Victor stood with his head in his hands. He had not anticipated this move and it had stopped a day's shooting as effectively as any damage to the pheasant stocks and woods. The pickup pulled back into the yard about ten minutes later; a dejected looking Robbie Landon got out and walked back towards the group who were now standing in the middle of the yard, many of whom were on mobile phones trying to arrange replacement tyres or some sort of recovery for their stranded vehicles.

"Sorry lads, they must have gone like the wind or I turned another way to them in the village; either way they've got away." They had done well to outpace Robbie in the lanes even with a slight start; it was an ongoing joke in the group that he was a bit of a mad driver despite his age and a lot of folks were not too keen on riding with him on shoot days.

It was mid afternoon by the time most of the vehicles were ready to roll again. Some of the day had been salvaged in the form of a duck drive at Brockleston Pits and a car had been despatched to the pub at lunch time to collect the hot pot; but it was all small recompense for what should have been, and the woods were left untouched that day. Even the usually flowing shoot conversation had more or less completely dried up by the time the group parted at around 3pm. None of them had any enthusiasm for the usual social gathering as the shoot day had not taken place. It was the most downhearted group of men and dogs ever to drive away from Brockleston Home Farm on a Saturday in winter.

✳ ✳ ✳ ✳ ✳

Nick Jones lay on the starched sheets of his hospital bed in the orthopaedic ward of Limcester General Hospital. His right leg had been badly broken in several places and he was awaiting surgery to pin it all back together. His right arm had already been placed in a plaster cast as it had a simple fracture. The pain was unbelievable;

the earlier morphine injection had long since worn off and the ward was so busy that he did not like to harass the nurses unless he had to; especially as he knew most of them through visiting accident victims there in the line of his work. He had only been at the hospital since about 11.30am that day but it seemed like weeks already. His only visitors had been his traffic sergeant and the duty inspector who had breathalysed him and officially revoked his police driving authority as a matter of course. They had asked him a lot of questions about how he had come to be colliding with a fully laden milk collection tanker whilst driving his own car on a country lane near Brockleston that morning, but had not really expressed any sympathy for him.

Nick had set off from home and headed towards Brockleston with his two dogs as usual. As he was approaching a left hand bend on a lane half way between Brocklesby and Brockleston a large steel field gate had suddenly swung out across his path from the nearside. He had reacted to the gate coming out at him and instinctively swerved to the offside, just as the tanker had approached from the other side of the bend. The lorry had been in its usual rush to complete its round of the local farms and Nick and his car had felt the full force of its weight coming towards them at 30 mph as the front off sides of the two vehicles met. Nick could not even remember the lorry, let alone the gate, when the two senior officers spoke to him. Nick had been trapped in his crumpled car and had to be cut out by the fire brigade before being transferred to Limcester General. At least the dogs were uninjured and his colleagues took the trouble to get them back home to his house. Neither Nick nor the tanker driver would have seen Elvis Hatton crouching in the field by the gate and then making off to the Green Renault Clio which had been pulled into a gateway a couple of fields away towards Brockleston. The two car occupants had then gone on to complete the second phase of that morning's mission at Home Farm. The oncoming tanker had been an added bonus; they had considered that the gate alone would have done enough damage to Nick's car to keep him away from the shoot, giving them a better opportunity to carry out their sabotage. Hampton and Hatton were in high spirits as they drove back to Limcester that morning; for the first time they had managed to stop a day's shooting at Brockleston and they had put a traffic cop in hospital which was by far the best part of it all for them. They stopped off at probably the only un-vandalised telephone box on Brandley Park on their way home and Hampton rang the mobile number they usually reported to. There was no answer and the call was switched to voicemail, "It's done, they won't be shootin' today." After leaving the message they drove on back to their flat, their good work done for the day.

At just after 4pm Nick was taken down to the operating theatre for the surgery on his leg. At least it's the start of the recovery, he thought to himself as he was wheeled down the corridor by a hospital porter with an appalling sense of humour, his jokes being only slightly less painful than the injuries. Nick was pretty apprehensive about it all, never having had anything like this happen to him before. It was all very well getting hardened to death, injury and destruction on the roads as a police officer; but dealing with other people was a whole lot different to having it happen to you. His thoughts soon ended as he drifted off quickly into a sweet anaesthetic induced oblivion.

✳✳✳✳✳

Victor had not managed to get the two tyres he needed for the Discovery brought out to the farm. He borrowed a small van from the estate yard and removed the Land Rover's wheels himself before taking them to a tyre fitter's on just the other side of Brocklesby. He hoped that the shoot's insurance would pay for the damage as Robbie had made a list of all the details before everyone left and was also going to make a single report to the police. He stopped off at the local village shop and post office in Brocklesby to buy a few groceries as the house was almost devoid of food. Whilst in the shop he picked up a copy of the local paper, considering it something to read that evening.

"How's this happened, who've you upset?" the tyre fitter commented as Victor stood around waiting as the work was carried out. He knew that to cut through a good tyre of a four wheel drive vehicle was no mean feat. Victor passed a quick remark regarding trouble on the shoot but did not really want to engage in too much conversation with the man. The least said about it all the better as far as he was concerned. He was also in a hurry to get back to Home Farm and replace his wheels. A late patrol of the woods was in his mind; if someone thought his vehicle was off the road it would be a tempting opportunity for more damage to be done. It was dark when Victor got back to Brockleston but he replaced the wheels on the Discovery by the light of the other vehicle's headlamps. He wasn't going to leave it there overnight. Changing the wheels on a Discovery is not the most effortless of tasks unaided and working half in the shadow cast by himself in the bright headlamps made it all the more difficult. It was some time before Victor was able to take the estate's vehicle back and then walk back to Home Farm before driving back to his cottage.

After eating Victor sat in the armchair by the fire; he picked up the copy of the *Limcester Chronicle* and tried to pick out something worth reading amongst the inane ramblings of local councillors vying for publicity on the run-up to yet another local election, and reports of women's institute meetings. As he was passing the announcements page a name jumped out at him:

## FLEMMING

### GEORGE WILLIAM

### 'BILL'

### AGED 74 YRS

It was old Bill Flemming. He had died at home earlier in the week. Victor stared at the few lines of the announcement in disbelief, re-reading it several times as the information sunk in. He could imagine Bill lying dead or dying in the flat whilst he had passed close by on his route to and from the game farm when he had collected the new feeders. He now bitterly regretted not stopping off to visit him, his preoccupation with the events at Brockleston taking precedence over taking a bit of time out to visit someone who had helped him out without question; someone that was in need of the company of his own sort and now another person that had left his life without him having the opportunity to say goodbye. The funeral was to be the following Thursday and Victor resolved to attend no matter what; as much now out of a sad sense of guilt as for his respect for one of the last survivors from a now rapidly fading era. Victor folded the newspaper and placed it on the floor next to the chair. He did not know what to think any more, let alone what to do. The only sound in the room was the relentless slow ticking of the clock, a ticking that reminded him that time was running out for him at Brockleston. The news of the day's disaster would be reaching Mowbray soon if it hadn't already. At least the agent had been away from Brockleston when it all occurred and was not likely to be contactable until the following day or even Monday but that was all just academic. He felt like ringing the agent himself straight away just to get it all over with but despite his feeling of loneliness he could not have really brought himself to speak to anyone let alone Mowbray. The problem of vehicle sabotage could easily be prevented in future by posting someone to watch over them; it would not be popular as people would have to miss out on some of the social pleasures of the shoot day but the need for it would be more than understood. It was the ongoing problem of what was going to happen next that was his real concern now. The woods and birds were not the only target for attention and it was clear that any path that was capable of causing disruption was going to be followed if available. He was far too agitated and depressed to settle and time itself appeared to have slowed down. His solitude bore down on him like a physical weight and he could not be bothered to even turn on the television or have a drink. He had not intended to go out until after midnight but by just after 11pm it had all got too much and he left the cottage, setting off for Home Farm in the Discovery. Something about the day's events and news had taken their toll and he had a feeling that his activities were becoming futile; he could not help thinking that he would be defeated in the end and he was only delaying the inevitable. He wished that Nick Jones had at least turned up that day. Even he appeared to have deserted him now.

He drove up to The Hall Wood and spent some time checking around the area before driving back down to the shoot shed where he parked in the yard and walked over to Brockleston Pits. The low quacking that was coming from the two pits reassured him that the ducks were still there and he did not approach closely for fear of disturbing them himself. As he approached the yard again and was just climbing over the style not far from where he had left the Land Rover, he heard a sound. It was like a chair being scraped across a stone floor. It was a sound that would have been unheard at other times but in the still silence of the night Victor's over active ears picked it up. He walked slowly around to the door of the shed. As he was passing the windows he saw a flicker of light from inside. His heart sank; someone must have set fire to the shoot shed. He hurried to the door and reached for the key; it wasn't there, the ledge was empty. He tried the door and it was unlocked. As he swung it open he saw a candle flame flickering up in the top right hand corner of the shed. It was burning in an iron candle holder that had been left there from a previous ladies' day; one of the guns had brought it in to decorate the place for the wives who attended on this one day each season. A figure sat in the corner next to the flame. Victor reached for a beater's heavy stick that was lying by the door as the figure got up and started towards him.

"Who's that, what do you want?" came the gruff voice from the semi darkness. Victor recognised it immediately and loosened his grip on the stick. It was Harry Black. Victor identified himself and both men laughed with relief.

"What the hell are you doing Harry? You scared me to death. I thought they'd torched the place."

"Sorry Vic, I had a right row with the wife and I just walked out and ended up at Home Farm so I thought I would sit in here for a bit; I thought they'd turned up for more too." Victor went over to the cupboard and took out a half full bottle of port. He pulled two glasses out of a cardboard box by the sink and walked up to where the candle was burning. He sat down in the corner, placing the glasses on the table in front of him, and poured out two very large measures of the dark red liquid from the dusty bottle.

"Sit down Harry and have one of these with me; it's nice to know there's someone just as miserable as me around tonight."

"I can't believe what happened today, who do you think's doing it?"

"Probably a pair from Limcester, Nick Jones reckons anyway, but apparently they don't sound the type to be just doing it for the sake of it; there's got to be someone behind it all." The two sat and talked for about half an hour; a second round of port was poured to keep out the cold.

"Well I'm going off to check the other woods, Harry. Can I give you a lift back into the village?"

"You can do better than that; I'll come with you and we'll check them together." As they drove off towards Lady Jane's Moss Victor told Harry the news of Bill Flemming's death. Harry hadn't known Bill but had heard a lot about him, mainly from Victor himself.

Harry had been seriously ill the year before with a form of cancer and Victor did not want to impose a long walk on him especially as, to his knowledge, the old beater had already walked at least from the village to Home Farm and possibly further. He knew from experience how the distance was just not noticed when you were angry and depressed. He decided to just check the outskirts of the woods on foot and leave Harry with the Discovery to guard it; this was very welcome as he had sustained enough potential expense regarding the damage to his vehicle already that day. They made their way slowly from The Moss through Old Jack's Slang to The Long Gorse and then on to Solomon's Wood. All seemed alright with the drives and it was pleasant having Harry's company. There had been many occasions in the shoot shed when the guns and their guests had gone into one of their closed discussions and the old beaters like Harry had been the only source of company for Victor. He was convinced that nothing was really meant by this occasional social apartheid and it was just probably the result of alcohol fuelled insensitivity, but at times it was a little hard to tolerate it even so. They cut across country to Graves Spinney, the only wood left to check. For once Victor was not hoping to hear the sound of an alarm mine from the wood or there being any sign of persons in the area. He did not want to take Harry Black that far into his confidence just yet. He was keeping what lay in Graves Spinney to himself as long as he could. When he checked the pen area there had not even been the now expected visit from a fox and he was soon back in the Discovery with Harry. It was around 2.30am by the time they had completed their tour of the woods and drove out onto Church Lane heading back towards the village. As they approached the junction with the Brockleston Road a vehicle turned into the lane; the full beam of its headlamps dazzled them as it headed towards them. The vehicle then stopped and reversed at speed back up the lane towards the junction, its lights still on full. It took off again along the Brockleston Road, heading out of the village in the direction of Limcester. They saw it was a fairly small car but could not have described it any further. They were still seeing its lights against their retinas for several minutes after it had left.

"Courting couple or something more suspicious."

"Something more suspicious, Harry, I think; even a man with someone else's wife with him isn't usually that reckless." Victor cursed to himself, the one place he wanted them to visit and he had scared them off. They really did have the luck of the devil at times. He turned onto the Brockleston Road himself, heading into the village to drop Harry off. He thanked him for his company as they parted. No doubt Harry's wife would be sound asleep by now and he doubted his story to her in the morning would not be believed; there weren't too many loose women in Brockleston to entertain a man of Harry's age on a Saturday night, thought Victor.

# *Chapter Ten*

C HOKING RED DUST FLEW UP in clouds from the leading vehicle as the two Verwond Voet Land Rovers sped along the dusty track back towards the lodge. It was early afternoon and the South African heat was just bearable for Hugo and Johnnie. The last morning's hunting had been spent tracking a herd of Zebra but the beasts had been elusive and no shots had been fired. This had been some relief to Hugo as he had been dreading actually looking through the rifle sights at one of the black and white animals; they were too much like horses for him to feel comfortable about shooting one of them. It had been an inauspicious end to what had been a successful week's sport for the two Englishmen. They had no complaints about their trip and even the slightly reticent Hugo had to admit that he had enjoyed the experience. Pieter and Johann brought the vehicles to a halt in the yard and the hunting party disembarked to prepare for lunch. The Van Hoek brothers apologised for the lack of success but Hugo would have none of it and thanked them for their efforts during the previous week.

Half an hour later the party sat in the cool of the dining room, sheltered from the harsh afternoon sun. As was traditional at Verwond Voet, Anna had prepared a sumptuous farewell meal, this was probably as much to encourage hunters to return again the following year as anything else; but the Kudu steaks tasted just as good no matter what the purpose of the excessive hospitality. There was a particularly impressive selection of Eastern Cape red wines to accompany the meat and the combination of midday alcohol and delicious food encouraged some very relaxed and friendly conversation between the Van Hoeks and their guests. It was a rare event to have genuine old English aristocracy seated in the dining room of the lodge and as the conversation steered itself effortlessly towards Hugo's ancestral home, Frans became more and more intrigued with the history of the estate and the sporting activities there.

"You and your sons must come over in January, Frans, we can put you up at the Hall and we will have a day at Brockleston. You can experience English driven pheasants firsthand." The invitation was accepted before the words faded on Hugo's lips; it was the closed season for Verwond Voet and so it was ideal for the Van Hoek family to take a trip to England then. It was at this moment that Hugo decided that he would spend the rest of the winter at Brockleston and have a traditional Christmas there for the first time in many years. The meal went on until late in the afternoon, far longer than had been planned. Hugo and Johnnie had intended to rest before they left for Port Elizabeth to catch their connecting flight to Cape Town; the couple of hours' sleep went out of the window along with the organising of the transport of trophies back to England. Frans agreed to send the trophies on to Roland Ward at his own expense in gratitude for Hugo's invitation and half an hour later the Mercedes hurriedly departed for the airport, the bones of both Englishmen's right hands still feeling as if they had been crushed by the powerful enthusiastic farewell handshakes of the South Africans.

Many hours and several thousand miles later the Boeing 747 began its final descent into Heathrow. A grey wet November morning greeted Lord Brockleston and his travelling companion as the airliner emerged from the base of the thick cloud layer seconds before it made contact with the airport's runway. As he walked down the aisle towards the exit door Hugo had brief second thoughts about his previous decision and wondered if he really would be better joining Johnnie Marchington on the next leg of his journey back to Nassau. The two friends parted in the terminal building and Johnnie went off to find his connecting flight. Hugo was relieved to think that he would not be flying further that day and was looking forward to a short stay in the capital with Jane before going on to Brockleston.

Hugo was met by a very excited and emotional Jane at the barrier as he wheeled his suitcase along amidst the group of latest arrivals at Heathrow. The Africa trip had been the first time that the two had been separated for more than a few hours since meeting up nearly two years ago. The past week had seemed a lot longer for Jane than it had for Hugo and he thought that she was never going to let go of him as she held him tightly in a crushing embrace before eventually relaxing her grip and letting him breathe again.

"Blimey old girl, you've missed me then, have you?" Hugo's broad grin gave away his own delight as Jane slapped him playfully on the arm in a mock rebuke for his teasing. They went by taxi to the central London hotel that Jane had booked for them and after checking in they indulged in an hour of intense passionate afternoon lovemaking before collapsing into the deep satisfied sleep of blissful exhaustion. The week's separation had added a little extra spark to their already powerful feelings for each other.

$$*****$$

Victor sat on the dry leaf litter that formed a light brown carpet under the trees of Lady Jane's Moss, his back resting against the trunk of a stunted oak as he gazed silently across to the other side of the ride where Storm was buried. There were few thoughts running through his mind as he passed the quiet Sunday afternoon in the woodland solitude. Rather than sit in the cottage or the 'Brockleston Arms' he had just gone out walking; he could have convinced himself that he had arrived at the spot merely by chance but his inner thoughts told him otherwise. Since an early age he had been convinced there was some hidden force or pattern in his life that decreed he was destined to be alone with his thoughts. Growing up in a fairly isolated village and with his father's belief that young Victor should always be engaged in some useful work on the estate or the shoot had meant that he had little interaction with others his age apart from when he was in school. Weekends and school holidays were more times of work than leisure and it was a rare event for him to visit a friend's house or for them to visit him. As a result he had become a quiet boy, not shy but awkward in new company due to his enforced isolation. It was only in his time at college that he had grown up, gaining the confidence to run his own life and interact with others. He had never had a large circle of friends but liked to have people around him that he valued and respected, those he regarded as worth knowing. For some reason that he could never understand he would always end up walking alone in the woods. He could remember doing it as a boy on Sunday afternoons when even his father allowed him some leisure time; he was now doing exactly the same thing all those years later. The pattern of his life was still there; Susan had gone, Sarah had gone and now even old Storm was not around. He enjoyed the quiet reassurance of the familiar surroundings but still felt the need for company and he knew that whatever happened fate was going to leave him alone with his thoughts in the end. Solitary meals and long empty nights were now all too familiar to him.

His ears were picking up nearly every little sound in the wood from the shriek of a pheasant to the rustle of dead leaves as thrushes hopped around the floor under the branches. He was suddenly aware of the approach of footfalls from further down the ride. Instinctively he drew back into the undergrowth to hide his presence and observe the intruders. A few minutes later the forms of Hampton and Hatton passed by on the ride. It was the first time he had got a clear view of the two and he had no doubt as to who they were, he could feel his hatred for them burning in every cell of his being. He could not make out what they were saying but heard them both laughing as they passed Storm's grave; the anger in him nearly boiled over at the thought of them mocking him in his own woods. He let the two pass and then followed their progress silently as he followed them down the wood from the cover of the trees. They made their way out of the wood and struck off across the fields towards the back of the church. Victor waited for several minutes before leaving the wood himself and making directly for the cover of Old Jack's Slang. Darkness was falling and afforded Victor some concealment as he crossed the open field by the shortest route and then turned towards the church, keeping within the lee of the two small coverts. He could see the pair heading behind the church and turning North East; they could only have been heading for Graves Spinney he thought. His heart started to pound with anticipation at the thought of the hateful pair in the bottom of the concealed pit as he crept through the boundary hedge of the churchyard to take a tactical short cut towards the wood through its ancient gravestones. He waited in the cover of the hedge overlooking the wood as Hampton and Hatton approached the spinney. He watched the two enter the tree line and allowed them a few minutes to get clear of the boundary before crossing the open field into the cover of Graves Spinney himself. Darkness had fallen properly by this time and it was hard to see in the gloom of the wood when he first entered. He could hear voices up ahead of him and knew he was heading in the right direction. The distinctive sound of a shotgun cartridge discharging rang out through the wood. Victor quickened his pace, heading towards the pen area at the sound of the alarm mine firing. He had got at least one of them, he grinned to himself in grim satisfaction. Just as he reached the clearing of the pen he felt a sudden pain across his face as a heavy fist made contact with his jaw, its force being magnified by his own speed towards it. At the same time he was knocked sideways by heavy shoulders barging past him and he fell winded onto the floor of the wood. The blackness grew even darker as his consciousness faded into the gloom of the wood and he was left lying oblivious at the edge of the clearing. It was several minutes before Victor's senses registered anything, then as the soothing hands of unconsciousness relaxed their grip and the harsh throbbing pain in his jaw asserted itself, he heard a low moaning sound coming from the direction of the pheasant pen. He was convinced there were two figures that had run past him before he was knocked into oblivion but even so he doubted he was imagining the sounds he could hear. He struggled slowly to his feet, still feeling unsteady and wincing at the harsh pains in his jaw and ribs. He made his way cautiously toward where the pit lay; the moaning sounds were still drifting towards him on the still air. He crouched on the edge of the trap; he could see a large hole at the side closest to the feed hoppers, with broken pieces of wood sticking out at the edges. He had no torch with him and it was impossible to see into the blackness below.

"Who's down there?" he called down into the darkness. A pained muffled voice answered from the depths of the pit; it sounded familiar. It was Harry Black.

"My leg's broke Vic, can you get me out?" Victor froze; it was the last voice he was expecting to hear.

"What the hell are you doing here Harry?"

"I was just out for a walk; we had another row. Thought I would have a look round for you." Victor pulled himself together, thinking fast.

"I will go and get the Land Rover and something to get you

out with; hang on I won't be long" Victor turned and started to head away.

"Fetch an ambulance, I'm in agony," Harry's words faded on the air as the gamekeeper hurried away.

It was about half an hour later that Victor returned to the pit with a ladder and a torch; he had managed to get the Discovery up close to the pen area after negotiating the narrow ride. He shone the light down into the pit and saw the agonised expression of Harry staring back at him; the old beater looked ashen and pained.

"Soon have you out Harry, just hang on." Victor pulled back some of the covering of the pit to make a hole big enough to work through before carefully lowering down the ladder and descending into the peaty prison. Harry's right ankle was badly swollen and deep purple bruising was already developing. Victor felt terrible guilt at being the author of Harry's pain, but was determined not to let it show and reveal the true nature of what the old man had fallen into. Harry's screams of pain were enough to wake the ancient dead of the spinney as Victor struggled to get him up the ladder, helping him hop up the rungs with his good ankle like some bizarre pantomime parrot. He eventually got Harry into the passenger seat of the Land Rover and they set off down the ride with the casualty moaning at every rut they passed over. They got to the village and Victor suggested they stop off at Harry's house to let his wife know what had happened, but Harry insisted on going straight to the accident and emergency department at Limcester General.

"What the hell happened Vic, where did that big hole come from?" It was obvious that Harry had not observed the nature of the pit and its concealment and Victor was not going to enlighten him.

"I don't know Harry, but that old spinney is just a big old peat bog, so perhaps the soil washed away from underneath." The old man seemed happy with this explanation as they drove through the night to Limcester.

"You didn't happen to see anyone else in the wood did you Harry?" "No, was there someone about, Vic?"

"I thought I heard someone earlier, that's all." They drove in silence until they entered the grounds of the hospital; Harry's pain was obviously keeping him occupied. The hospital staff took Victor to task over transporting Harry himself, but he was able to pass it off saying that it was far more efficient to have done what he had due to where Harry had been found. He knew that wide awake paramedics or fire and rescue personnel would have had no problems in observing the unusual nature of what Harry had fallen into and it was the last thing he wanted. Harry was taken straight through to a treatment room as the department was unusually quiet and Victor took a seat in the waiting room. A short time later a doctor came out to Victor and questioned him about how Harry had come by his injury.

"Sounds like a dangerous place, this Brockleston Shoot," he commented. Victor questioned the doctor about his remark and was told that someone had been involved in a road accident on their way to the shoot the day before. It did not take Victor long to work out that it must have been Nick Jones, explaining the policeman's uncharacteristic absence. He started to ask the doctor questions about it but was refused any answers as a matter of standard procedure. The doctor then went back into the department; about half an hour later a nurse came out to tell him that Harry was comfortable but had a fairly complex fracture of his ankle and they would be keeping him in and transferring him to a ward. Victor felt a pang of guilt, especially knowing that Harry had only just recently suffered a great deal with his illness. He paid a brief visit to Harry before leaving the hospital and told him that he would visit his wife on the way home to tell her what had happened. Harry grabbed his arm and insisted that he didn't, saying that he would ring her himself to explain. This surprised Victor but he thought nothing of it; it was probably best to stay out of it all, especially if the two had been having arguments already.

Victor drove quickly back to Brockleston. The differential of the old Discovery whined its protest as he gunned the vehicle's unwieldy bulk down the empty lanes. He had a lot of urgent business to attend to back in Graves Spinney. He spent several frenzied hours clearing the site of the old carpet and the entire wooden frame, which he had to saw into lengths to fit in the Land Rover. He used an old besom to brush away any spade marks he had made around the pit before brushing leaves into it and spreading them around as if they had just fallen in. It wasn't that convincing he thought but it was a lot less obvious than it had been a few hours earlier.

It was just after 1.30am by the time he had emptied all the debris into the old shed at Keeper's Cottage and he then collapsed in the chair by the old cooker, completely exhausted, both physically and mentally. His whole body seemed wracked with pain from his jaw to his aching ribs and through to his over taxed muscles from hours of frenzied activity. He was too tired to be bothered moving and afforded himself one of the few luxuries of living alone; he spent the night in the chair by the warmth of the cooker.

# *Chapter Eleven*

"**W**HAT THE HELL HAPPENED TO you?" Robbie Langdon stood at the door of Keeper's Cottage staring incredulously at the bruised and swollen jaw that hung at the bottom of Victor's face. It was 10.30am and Victor had slept on into the morning oblivious of the time. He had been awakened by Robbie's knocking and made his way slowly and painfully to the door. The keeper ushered the captain into the cottage and tried to spark up the cooker without success before reverting to the rarely used electric kettle. Robbie had got to hear about Harry Black's injury and had come to hear the full story from the keeper. Victor started to relate his version of events to Robbie as the kettle performed its task. The kitchen was as cold as the grave and Victor shuddered even though he was still wearing his outside clothes from the night before. The early morning November chill had eaten into his bones after the warming fire in the cooker had faded to an ember as he slept. He felt too exhausted and pained to feel the usual embarrassment of being caught asleep at that time of the day and Robbie was too busy expressing his sympathy for it to be an issue with the shoot captain in any case. After he had placed the steaming cups of coffee down on the table in the cold kitchen Victor reached for a whisky bottle and poured a couple of measures into each mug, more to ward off his own agonies than as an act of country hospitality.

"Well you're up against it and no mistake Vic; have you told the police about last night?"

"Not yet, no, I haven't really had the chance and I doubt it would achieve anything by what Nick Jones has told me." Victor then told Robbie about what he had learned the night before at the hospital about Nick.

"Well Mowbray is going to be making more noise than ever now, especially as Lord Hugo is back in England and intends to be here for the winter." Victor could not believe his ears; as if things were not already bad enough, the return of Lord Brockleston would mean added pressure for him as Mowbray would be constantly on his back trying to impress his Lordship no doubt.

"When is his Lordship due to arrive?"

"This next weekend, he's staying up in London until then." Robbie thanked Victor for the coffee and left as quickly as he had appeared, leaving Victor to ponder his increased pressures.

Victor's first port of call after a few slices of toast and more coffee was Graves Spinney. He was anxious to see the pit in daylight. It did not look too bad he thought, it was at least a natural feature to start with and he had only adapted it for his own ends. A good heavy downpour would complete his re-naturalisation of it and in a typical English winter heavy rain was never too far way. There was a half full can of petrol lying by one of the feeders and its intended purpose for burning them was only too obvious; the plastic hoppers and wooden frames would have burned easily after being doused with the fuel. He may not have caught his prey but at least he had prevented more damage for the time being, he thought. The intensity of the attacks had reached new heights with this attempt following hard on the heels of Saturday's tyre slashing. There would be no let up by the look of it. He topped up the hoppers and placed the petrol can in the Discovery before driving off to check the rest of the shoot. He was relieved to find no further signs of sabotage across the rest of the woods and drives, but it was only a small compensation when compared with the increased pressure he was now under. He would normally have found the prospect of Lord Hugo returning to the estate very satisfying; but under the prevailing circumstances it felt like the imminent arrival of a final judgement, perhaps the beginning of the last chapter for the Brockleston Shoot.

Victor arrived back at the cottage in the early afternoon. There was a note pinned to the cottage door. It was from Mowbray; the agent wanted to see him regarding Lord Hugo's visit. Victor took a brief lunch break at the cottage before driving to the estate office.

"We need to put a good show on this Saturday, Drew; his Lordship is going to attend to see how it's shaping up and he's planning on having his own guests attending later in the season."

Victor's heart sank at the words that Mowbray was spouting across the old oak desk towards him. He just nodded and said that he would try his hardest to put a good day on, despite his fears. The only good news for Victor was that the imminent arrival of Lord Hugo had spurred Mowbray into providing some assistance to the keeper from the estate workforce; two of the maintenance staff were to be put at his disposal for the rest of the week. John Wrench and Arthur Young both lived in tied cottages in the village and would prove very useful to him in the next few days. Victor for once was highly grateful to Mowbray despite the fact that the agent had no other real option due to Lord Hugo's visit. The meeting with Mowbray had not been all bad and Victor's spirits felt slightly uplifted as he made his way to the workshops on the other side of the estate yard to speak with John and Arthur. They had been expecting him when he walked into the joiner's shop. The distinctive smell of freshly brewed strong tea and the sweet essence of pine sap, mixed with the countless other aromas of wood preservers and paints, welcomed him into the dusty but homely workshop. Both men were sitting on an old church pew against the wall next to the ancient iron potbellied stove that was just inside the doorway, its metal glowing red in places as it consumed its constant supply of scrap wood from joinery projects. For Victor it was like going back in time to his childhood. Memories of cold, wet winter afternoons spent sheltering in the workshop with now long dead estate workers flooded back. He still recalled their kindly faces and their hospitality, always pleased to receive visitors and take a break from the monotony of producing windows, doors and other joinery items required for the estate properties. Arthur Young poured Victor a cup of the dark brown brew from a white enamelled billycan which was stained by decades of good Indian leaf; Victor smiled to himself as he wondered if it would have been possible to produce a good cup of tea from the can without even bothering to put in any fresh leaves at all. The keeper got down to the business in hand; he could see that the two men were keen to help and their escape into the open air was to be a welcome break from the workshop. Both men were in their mid 40s and had spent most of their lives on the estate. They had attended the shoot as beaters when required in the past and no doubt got up to all manner of activities in the local countryside during their formative years; so Victor had no need to outline the geography of the area or describe the layout of the shoot to them. The meeting was more of an informal discussion or debate than a giving of direct orders. Victor had not gone to the workshop with any preconceived ideas. He had not had time to formulate any plan and even if he had he would have consulted the two men about it in any case. He had no desire to alienate anyone; he had few enough allies as it was. In the end it was decided that Arthur would patrol an area to the west of an imaginary line running through St John's Church and south along the Brocklesby Road; this would take in Solomon's Wood, The Long Gorse, Old Jack's Slang and The Moss, the remainder of the area to the east of this line being covered by John. Both men would work between 10am and 6pm patrolling the shoot, topping up feeders and carrying out routine repairs as required; this would leave Victor to cover the unsociable hours and rest during the day if he needed to. The thought of removing some of the physical exhaustion from his life for a few days was a great relief to Victor; he left the workshop feeling a lot less alone than he had done for some time. The imminent arrival of Lord Hugo had prompted Mowbray into helping him out at last. The newly found assistance had also arrived just in time to allow Victor to leave Brockleston for long enough to keep an appointment that he had been torn over attending due to recent events.

\*\*\*\*\*

Victor walked slowly down the gravel path behind the little group of mourners following the simple coffin; it carried Bill Flemming on a last short journey to his final home in the little graveyard of Longacre Church. It had been a simple and short service. The young priest had been brought in from a group of neighbouring parishes as the old church was now rarely used for services. There were so few of the original village inhabitants left that it was not worth keeping the church fully open. Longacre was now more of a commuter suburb than a part of the countryside. The Reverend Miles Clark had done his best to give old Bill a fitting send-off but it was clear the young cleric knew very little of the man he was now guiding into eternity and even less about the path the old keeper had trod through his seven decades. The bearers struggled across the unkempt tussocky grass as they carried Bill to where an old family grave awaited him. It had been over 20 years since the earth there had been disturbed. An old headstone decorated with the ravages of moss and lichen bore witness to this. The last entrant had been Bill's wife Dorothy, taken from him all too early in her life by cancer. Victor stood back, allowing the undertakers and the few close family Bill had to gather at the graveside. Looking out of the churchyard he could see the neatly manicured expanse that was the Longacre Golf Course where Bill had spent his last years doing a poor substitute for his past occupation. The moles would no longer be troubled by the cold steel grip of his traps. It was a cold and grey late November afternoon. The meagre light had already started to fade as the featureless clouds thickened with the threat of rain. There was not an ounce of cheer or hope to be grasped upon as Victor watched his old friend being lowered into the earth that they were both brothers to. It was an end of an era sort of scene with the dullness of the day adding heavily to the sadness that was welling up in Victor, a feeling that was difficult to keep respectfully hidden. He turned and walked slowly from the graveside, unable to face the customary introductions and commiserations, fearing that his outer composure would break down. He got into the Discovery and headed away just as the rain started to fall. There was little solace to be taken from the afternoon's event apart from the knowledge that Bill had been buried in ground familiar to him as he had wished. The old keeper had avoided the urban and anonymous end in the flames of the factory-like modern crematorium in Limcester, which had befallen many of the old country folk from the area. It was this irrational but strangely comforting thought that accompanied Victor on his journey back to Brockleston.

# Chapter Twelve

Hugo and Jane travelled to Limcester by train and were collected by car from the railway station.

"Typical English weather they've laid on for us."

"Yes your Lordship, it never improves much these days but they've given it taking up again overnight so it should be fine for tomorrow's shoot." The Daimler turned into Hall Lane off the Brockleston Road and headed towards the entrance of the family home, its driver Jim Reynolds increasing the speed of the windscreen wipers to counteract the sudden downpour. Jim was a quietly spoken man in his mid forties; Hugo's father had taken him on just before his death to manage the running of the house and to fill the roles of both valet and butler, functions that would at one time have been carried out by at least three separate staff members. Jim's predecessor, who had originally only filled the post of butler before taking on the combined roles during a spell of cost cutting at the hall, had retired after nearly 20 years of service with the family. Hugo had instantly taken to the man; his unassuming but confident manner was what he had come to expect of his staff over the years and Jim could be trusted completely with all aspects of his duties. The question of keeping Jim on when the hands on the reins of the estate changed was never an issue. The Daimler was a shining example of Jim's work; it had not been used by the family since the late Lord's funeral, but Reynolds had looked after and maintained it in excellent serviceable condition through all the time it had stood silently in the old coach house at the hall. The car came to a sedate halt on the freshly raked gravel outside the main entrance to the house. There was no group of faithful servants lined up outside the hall to greet the returning master as there had been in the old days; but Hugo felt comforted to see his old home again and was appreciative of Reynolds's attentions as Jane and he alighted from the car and went inside. There was now no full time staff at the hall apart from Jim Reynolds who lived in a small flat at the rear overlooking the kitchen garden. Agency cleaners were engaged to maintain the interior when required and the grounds were maintained by the estate workers under the direction of Mowbray. Despite the short notice the butler had got the Hall in splendid condition to welcome Lord Brockleston home; there were no lingering dust sheets covering the furniture and all the rooms had been freshly aired and cleaned to eliminate the musty smell of a house that has been closed up for far too long. A log fire blazed in the drawing room and tea and freshly baked scones appeared from the kitchen just as Reynolds was taking their coats out of the room. Annie Lewis, the former cook at the Hall, had been persuaded to come out of retirement to prepare food for their stay. Now in her late sixties, the plump, red-faced woman had been overjoyed at the chance of returning to her former domain to provide for Hugo and Jane and any of their guests at the Hall in the coming weeks. Annie was the classic image of the traditional family cook and Jane smiled to herself with charmed amusement as the silver tray was brought in and placed on the table in front of them.

"Mrs Lewis, you even remembered my liking for your marvellous cherry scones."

"Some things can't be forgotten; welcome home, Lord Hugo, and you too, Miss Rotherby-Hyde. I'm happy to be back here for a while." Hugo could tell the greeting was heartfelt and he was slightly embarrassed at her servitude. Such respect and reverence seemed a bit out of place now after all the years, especially coming from a woman so many years his senior, even in that drawing room with its old décor and furnishings so far removed from the modern outside world.

Hugo and Jane were still taking their afternoon tea when Reynolds returned.

"Is everything to your liking Sir?"

"Reynolds I'm speechless, thank you, you've done much more than expected." The butler clearly hesitated for a few seconds, looking uncomfortable; Hugo assumed it was perhaps the compliment that had caused some embarrassment.

"Sir, about the baggage, where would you like me to put it?" Hugo realised the cause of Reynolds' hesitation, a delicate question in the eyes of his servant that had to be asked; he was tactfully referring to the sleeping arrangements. Despite his modern lifestyle, Hugo too felt some embarrassment; back in Brockleston the carefree reality of the Bahamas and London seemed out of place.

"Put mine in my old room; they're the green canvas ones, and put Miss Rotherby-Hyde's in the room opposite, mother's old room, thank you Reynolds." There was no need to subject his staff to the realities of modern life too blatantly; the token gesture of apparent separate sleeping accommodation was the decent solution he had thought after a few seconds of private deliberation.

"Very good sir." Both men silently asked themselves who they thought they were fooling as Reynolds went to the car to collect the luggage from the Daimler's ample boot.

About an hour after his Lordship's arrival Mowbray arrived at the Hall. He was wearing a new suit and his vehicle had been freshly washed; the accumulated Brockleston mud of the previous few weeks had been removed that morning by one of the estate workers that the agent had used for the task. He strode up the short flight of stone steps to the great oak door and pressed the antique white porcelain button set in the polished brass surround on the wall. The deep tone of the old bell sounded in the servants' hall and the butler made his way from his flat to answer the door.

"Mr Mowbray, Sir."

"Show him in please Reynolds." The beaming agent entered the drawing room. His stage-managed greeting annoyed Hugo, but he was too polite to let it show. After the customary pleasantries and a short report regarding the general running of the estate, the agent came to the business of the shoot; he told his Lordship of the recent problems and his assigning of the two estate workers to the keeper to strengthen security.

"Good man, but do you think that's enough Richard? These buggers can be pretty determined you know. I've read some awful reports in the press in the last year; they seem to have stepped up their campaign since the hunting ban."

"Well the whole shooting scene in the country is on a bit of a knife edge at the moment sir. I'm starting to wonder if it sits with sound business these days, too many unpredictable parts to the whole equation now; the estate is carrying it for the most part as it is."

"Hmm, not what I wanted to hear really. I love coming back

here and seeing it as it should be; but as you say it's probably not sensible; still we'll see how we go on; it would be a shame to part with one of the last remnants of a very long tradition and in any case we've the rest of this season to enjoy I hope."

"Will you be shooting tomorrow sir?" asked Reynolds.

"Hadn't thought of that. Yes, why not? Give Robbie Langdon a call for me later, will you Richard? See if it's convenient; let me know if it isn't." This was really a token remark as it was written into the contract of the shoot that his Lordship and his guests could avail themselves of shooting whenever required. Mowbray took his leave and left the hall.


"Perhaps sir would like to inspect the gun room and select a sporting piece for tomorrow." It was a well rehearsed and much loved question and Hugo accompanied Reynolds to the small locked room at the end of the hallway with as much hidden pleasure as his butler. Although not as impressive as the collections at some of the more noted sporting estates, the guns at Brockleston Hall were not inconsequential. The jewel in the collection was a beautiful pair of antique Purdeys that had been made for Hugo's grandfather, a reminder of the great sporting past. In total there were a dozen shotguns of different types and ages with a similar number of sporting rifles of assorted calibres; the weapons adorned the walls of the room, leaving just enough space for an ammunition cabinet and a small green leather topped table in the centre of the room which held neatly arranged gun cleaning and maintenance items.

"It's a credit to you Reynolds, like the rest of the place." After an appreciative look around the racks, Hugo selected an English side by side 26 inch barrelled twelve bore, a traditional game gun.

"That will do fine; we won't be doing mass slaughter, will we? Brockleston doesn't hold the game that it once did," Hugo said with mild amusement as he ran his fingers over the fine walnut stock of the weapon before mounting it to his shoulder.

# Chapter Thirteen

THE USUAL COLLECTION OF VEHICLES was arrayed in the yard at Home Farm as Mowbray drove in with Lord Hugo in the passenger seat of his Freelander. The guns and beaters had all arrived a few minutes early that morning at Robbie Langdon's request for a pre-briefing regarding giving his Lordship a good day. Robbie realised that the shoot was under threat, having taken notice of Mowbray's recent comments to him and the events of the past few weeks. He wanted to keep his Lordship `on side` by giving him the best day possible. Robbie had consulted with Victor over the best peg for each of the drives and they had made sure Hugo was going to get placed on most of these by fixing the draw for places; sporting fairness had been traded for common sense in a good cause. Victor was in a fairly relaxed mood for once; he was pretty sure the shoot had been saved from interference over the past few days due to his recent increase in assistance and even the weather was good for a change. It was a bright, clear morning with just a hint of frost and it was forecast to stay dry for a few days. Bill Stewart at the pub had been instructed to make sure the hot pot was above even his usually high standard and had also been authorised to provide a decent cheeseboard and some good wine to complement it. These additions were coming out of the captain's own pocket; if he could save the shoot by laying out a few extra quid it was money well spent in his opinion.

Victor was standing by the game racks when Hugo entered the shoot shed.

"Good morning, Your Lordship, great to see you again."

"And to see you too Victor; I see you've even managed to arrange the weather." Hugo circulated around the shed, shaking hands and greeting gun and beater alike. Mowbray was at his heels trying in vain to steer his Lordship in the direction of the `better members and guests` with very limited success. Lord Brockleston was the first in the book for the day's sweepstake and put down a high number of birds, far more than had been shot on any day that season. David Radford wrote it on one of the old yellowed pages of his notebook without comment and thanked him as he dropped the coins into the cup of his thermos flask that he always used to collect the stake money. Robbie and Victor had already worked out the battle plan for the day and they were determined to provide as good a day's shooting as possible from what was available. Robbie went through the drives for the morning before the party went out to the vehicles and moved off towards the village.

The column of vehicles left the Brockleston Road near Lady Jane's Moss and headed cross country towards the outskirts of the Long Gorse, where Victor arranged the guns in an arc at the southern end of the wood, covering half of its circumference. Hugo was placed in the centre of the line, directly beneath the point where the majority of the pheasants usually flew out as they headed for the refuge of Graves Spinney. A few minutes later Victor nodded to Robbie Langdon, who was with the beaters that day, and the captain blew his whistle to signal the start of the drive. The beating line entered the northern end of the wood and formed an even line across the width of The Gorse. Victor told them to move off. There was no sign of any birds for the first 50 yards, but then a covey of three birds rose from in front of one of the spaniels and rocketed skyward, climbing above the trees and heading in the direction of the spinney.

"Birds forward!" The three pheasants covered the length of the wood and emerged over the guns, just within range of Lord Brockleston, side by side. Hugo was taken by surprise; it was a long time since he had swung a shotgun through the line of a high bird and he rushed his first uncoordinated shot, missing the lead bird by several feet, a feat he repeated with his second barrel on the same bird. These first two birds escaped unscathed towards Graves Spinney; the third, which was lagging behind, veered to Hugo's left and towards Charlie Davidson; it stood little chance as by that time in the season Charlie was always on top form and killed it with his first shot of the day. As soon as Charlie's bird had been picked up by an enthusiastic Labrador a second cry went up from the beating line and a fairly constant supply of birds then started to emerge over the waiting guns. As the mid morning sun shone down on that last Saturday in November, Hugo was too busy to worry about what birds he had missed and soon relaxed into the pleasure of the shooting, his aim improving as he did so and the day's bag being added to accordingly. Despite the Long Gorse being an outlying wood on the shoot, it was also one of the largest and it yielded up a tally of birds in proportion to its size that morning by the time Robbie Langdon blew his horn at the end of the drive. Forty three birds started off the day's total, a good many of which were accounted for by his Lordship.

Solomon's Wood was usually shot just before The Gorse, but it had been decided to leave it out that day. The earlier devastation of its release pen and pheasant stocks would have meant an unproductive drive for Lord Hugo no matter where they had stood him in the line. There were a reasonable number of pheasants held there by the new feeders but not enough to provide part of the quality of shooting day that was aimed for.

The next drive was to be at Old Jack's Slang. Victor had gone up to the two narrow woods with Robbie Langdon on the previous afternoon and they had driven the birds from the easterly half of the Slang across the narrow gap into the other half of the wood late in the day. This 'dogging in' with the help of the captain's two Labradors was intended to concentrate the pheasants in the far wood as most of them would remain there overnight to be driven back the following morning by the beaters. Hugo was positioned centrally in the gap between the two halves of the wood; if everything went to plan this would be the 'hot seat' for the drive. Most of the other guns were positioned on the flanks of the Slang up to about half way up the westerly wood, with two walking guns following up just behind the beaters to deal with any birds that flew back over the line. The drive was as successful as planned and Hugo was again treated to some excellent game in good numbers, including the bonus of two separate woodcock, one of which he killed with a second barrel, the other being too low flying to shoot at safely.

The final drive at The Moss was equally successful; this time the guns were lined up along the ride within the wood with Lord Hugo again in the centre of the line.

By the time the steaming hot pot and bread rolls were being served back at the shoot shed there were 130 birds hanging on the game racks, including three ducks and a woodcock amongst the pheasants. Hugo sat next to David Radford, enjoying the food, wine and conversation with the shoot members and guests. It had been a good morning and spirits were high; Mowbray had stayed on for the lunch; he had not been shooting but had remained with Hugo throughout the morning. His Lordship was obviously enjoying the day's sport and the agent had the good sense to leave the talk to shooting and countryside matters, rather than spoil it by bringing up the recent problems at Brockleston.

The afternoon's activities were to be centred closer at hand, in and around The Hall Wood; preceded by the duck drive at Brockleston Pits. Robbie and Victor were now fairly confident of a successful day as these drives had performed well so far that season and it would be easy to build on the productive morning. The guns got to their pegs at the pits and went `live` immediately in case the birds took to the air early before Victor disturbed them as planned. Hugo had been positioned on the Home Farm side of the pits, as usually at least some of the ducks flew in that direction when put up; although so far that season there had been fairly even spread over all the surrounding guns. The ducks took flight as soon as Victor started to approach the pits; most of them headed over Hugo, who was ready for them and managed a `left and right`, bringing down two of the Mallards before the great majority then passed over his empty gun as he struggled to re-load for further shots. Just a few other birds were bagged by the guns either side of Hugo. Just after the shooting at the pits stopped there were a few other bangs heard from the direction of The Hall Wood; at first it sounded like random isolated shots, then the intensity of the sounds increased, building to a cacophony like machine gun fire. It was like a Spanish fiesta when a town square exploded in a torrent of hanging firecrackers. Victor emerged from the slope at the side of the pits; he was staring with a look of disbelief towards the nearby wood. The noise went on for about five minutes, but it seemed like hours to the gamekeeper. Whatever it was it had probably put paid to any further pheasant drives that day. The few ducks that had been shot were picked up and the group walked to the vehicles to drive the short distance up to the wood. Victor was speechless; he couldn't believe that the day's fortunes had suddenly changed so dramatically. They drove to the farthest end of the wood and stopped the vehicles close to the ride there. Victor and Robbie hurried off into the wood, closely followed by Hugo and his agent, all equally keen to discover some sign of what had happened in the wood. They didn't need to look very hard; as they got just a few yards into the ride they saw that it had been the site of a sizeable firework display. Strings were tied at angles between the trees either side, spreading for about 50 yards down the wood. The burst and spent cardboard cases of the crackers hung from the strings and the floor of the ride was littered with the fragments of them. The acrid but sweet smell of gunpowder hung in the still air of the wood. "Well they've gone to some trouble here and no mistake; they've done it almost right under our noses too; they couldn't have left too long ago by the timing of this either." Robbie Langdon stared down the ride as he flicked the remains of one of the hanging cardboard cases. Victor sprinted off down the ride and out of the wood, leaving the others standing in the remains of the disturbance. He jumped into the driver's seat of his Land Rover and took off back down the track towards Home Farm. He struggled to keep the old Land Rover on a straight course as it bounced wildly down the track towards Home Farm, thrashing the old engine for all that it was worth as it slewed from side to side on the muddy track, at times barely maintaining traction as he over revved it in his efforts to drive at speed in a place where steady careful progress was usually the norm. He got to the road and made for the village, the Discovery's wheels spinning as they struggled to grip the hard surface, the tyres still clogged with accumulated mud. As the tread started to clear the progress became more stable and the gamekeeper increased the vehicle's speed to as fast as he dare drive in the narrow lanes; spurred on by his desire to meet the perpetrators of the latest outrage, this was a lot faster than he would normally have travelled. The junction with the Brockleston Road loomed up on him; he intended to slow as little as possible for the turn towards Limcester and positioned the Land Rover towards the nearside verge, intending to take a wide curve through the junction to keep his speed up. He leaned forward to get an early view of the road either side of the junction; a vehicle was coming from the right and he realised he would not get out before it arrived; he braked hard and the wheels locked, not helped by what remained of the mud in the tyre treads. The

Discovery slid out onto the Brockleston Road across the path of the oncoming car which also had to brake suddenly, its driver taken by surprise at the suddenly emerging Land Rover. The oncoming vehicle slammed into the driver's door of the Discovery, the force throwing Victor's upper body across into the front passenger seat. His legs hit the centre gear box cover and for a few seconds he was winded. He had not bothered to fasten his seat belt and there had been nothing to lessen his movement in the vehicle as he was thrown sideways. He heard the sound of the other car reversing and a screech of tyres as it turned and headed back the way it had come from along the Brockleston Road towards Limcester. Victor managed to get himself up into a sitting position; an intense pain shot through his lower back and hips as he did so, making him cry out. He looked down the road and there was no sign of the vehicle that he had pulled out on. He was expecting to be faced with an irate driver, clearly on the right side of the law as he had emerged from the give way junction right into the other vehicle's path. There was no sign of anything in the lane apart from some skid marks, broken headlamp glass and some mud dislodged from the underside by the impact. Victor got more of an impression of the other vehicle than a clear studied look at it. He had only seen it for a fleeting moment, but he was sure it had been an old Japanese four wheel drive vehicle either grey or light blue metallic in colour. In his mind he had the impression that the two people in its front seats were the ones that had knocked him down at Graves Spinney that night; but he dismissed this as fancy; if it had been them and they had just caused the disturbance that had caused him to drive the way he had, why were they headed back into Brockleston? A few minutes later as Victor was painfully getting out of the passenger seat of his damaged vehicle Mowbray's Freelander and Robbie Langdon's Pickup arrived at the junction.

"Are you alright Drew? You look like death, what the hell happened?" It was Hugo that spoke first, rushing past the agent and the captain in his concern for the gamekeeper. Despite the obvious grimace of pain Victor told them that he wasn't badly injured as he walked around the back of the damaged Land Rover to inspect the driver's side. The doors would not open and the sill was badly bent in, but the front wheel and wheel arch seemed intact; the vehicle was still driveable if not a bit inconvenient to use. Hugo insisted on driving the damaged car back to Keeper's Cottage and Mowbray followed in his own vehicle to pick him up and return his Lordship to the Hall afterwards.

"Now are you sure you're ok Drew?" Hugo helped the keeper out of Mowbray's Freelander and into the cottage. Victor insisted that he was alright and thanked Lord Brockleston for his time and trouble before collapsing painfully into the chair by the cooker.

# Chapter Fourteen

NICK JONES LAY ON THE settee inside the small tidy lounge of his modest semi-detached home gazing absently in the direction of the television set that his wife had switched on prior to her leaving for work. His two dogs sprawled across the carpet just beneath him, no doubt wondering why their master was lying around in the middle of the morning. Their excitement at his arrival back home the previous afternoon had now turned into a subdued resignation that he wasn't going to be taking them out for a run across the nearby fields anytime soon. The two Labradors were managing to make the best of it though, as always, making full use of their ability to almost sleep the clock round if any other activity was off the menu for the time being. The house was just too quiet. The monotonous banality of daytime television did nothing to occupy his thoughts and he had grown tired of reading for the sake of it. He hadn't heard from Victor since the keeper had briefly looked in on him at the hospital on the night following his accident and he had not been contacted by anyone else from the shoot; the most recent events at Brockleston were beyond his knowledge. It was going to be a long week and an even longer winter he thought to himself.

***** 

Harry Black's broken leg was not healing at all; his advanced age and his previous illness were no doubt contributing to his slow recovery from his injury. It looked as if he would be lucky to be out of Limcester General by Christmas; so he had plenty of time for contemplation as he lay in the austere surroundings of the orthopaedic ward. Harry's wife did not drive and his two daughters

120

were both long married with their own families and lived some distance away; so his visitors were few and far between.

\*\*\*\*\*

Hugo and Jane sat at the end of the great table in the dining room of the Hall having helped themselves to a late breakfast. Jim Reynolds had laid this out on the sideboard before he and Annie Lewis had driven off to Limcester to replenish the fresh food stocks. Hugo was unusually quiet. Jane remarked on this but he passed it off as tiredness; they had both over indulged at dinner the previous evening, Hugo especially so. They had invited Sir Jack Melton and his wife along with the Rotherby-Hydes to stay at the Hall for a few days as 'Jack's Comet' was running at the nearby Milthorpe Racecourse that afternoon. Sir Jack had insisted Hugo and Jane accompany them to the meeting, but Hugo had declined due to the pressing situation at Brockleston, although he had given Mowbray the day off to accompany the party to the course.

\*\*\*\*\*

Victor was in the yard at Keeper's Cottage, prising frantically at the stuck driver's door of the Discovery with a short crowbar. He had been out patrolling the woods all Sunday night and the early hours of that Monday morning and had grown seriously tired of having to get in and out of the front passenger door of the vehicle. He cursed as he missed the end of the bar with his hammer, striking the back of his hand. He was so tired his eyes hardly focussed but he was determined to have the door open before he went to bed that morning.

\*\*\*\*\*

Arthur Young busied himself checking and filling the hoppers of the feeders in Solomon's Wood; he worked slowly and methodically, stopping every few seconds to listen to the woods around him. He was ill at ease, a state of mind that was very foreign to him, especially in such familiar surroundings. He knew that he was nearly on the edge of the estate, in the wood furthest from Brockleston Village and any semblance of nearby assistance. He knew that John Young was likely to have started his working day in The Hall Wood, concentrating his efforts there to try to address the disturbance to the birds on the last shoot day as per Victor's instructions. The thought of how far he was likely to be from his work colleague did nothing to ease his thoughts.

✷✷✷✷✷

Hampton and Hatton were both sound asleep in the fragrant confines of their Brandley Park flat; the contents of the brown envelope that had been dropped through their door early on Sunday morning had been made good use of at the local off-licence. They had little memory of the day before and even less regard for it.

# *Chapter Fifteen*

Victor's efforts with the hammer and crow bar not only resulted in a badly bruised and swollen left hand, but also achieved the practical end of allowing him once again the use of the Land Rover's driver's door. The make shift repair was not aesthetically pleasing but it made life a lot easier on his nightly patrols of the woods during the rest of the week. He was convinced something else was going to be damaged, killed or interfered with before the next shoot; however his fears appeared unfounded, although as Saturday drew nearer his concerns increased again as they always did. His Lordship had no plans to join the party again that weekend as he was entertaining his guests still; but there was no doubt that Hugo would still be very interested in how things went even so. Victor had paid particular interest to every strange car he had seen in the area that week, convinced that the four wheel drive that had nearly wrecked his Discovery would have now been replaced by something else. More than once he had been stared at by the occupants of passing cars due to his obvious interest in them and there were two occasions when drivers wound down their windows and hurled abuse at him. Both Robbie Langdon and Richard Mowbray had been constant visitors to the cottage that week wanting reports of any happenings, but neither Victor nor his two assistants had seen or found anything untoward. It was as if his tormentors were taking a break to celebrate their recent success. As it turned out Saturday's shoot passed without incident and a decent size bag was recorded in the game book. John Young had done well in The Hall Wood and the number of birds, although slightly down on previous weeks, were respectable there. The shoot went on to run well throughout December as the winter drew on and Christmas approached.

"Looks like you scared the buggers off, Drew, when they ran into you." Hugo leaned across the table in the shoot shed and poured yet another large shot of whisky into Victor's still half full glass.

"Well perhaps Your Lordship, I certainly hope so." It was the last Saturday before Christmas and Lord Brockleston had joined the shoot that afternoon, walking with the beating line and being thoroughly sociable with all present. For the previous fortnight Hugo had been constantly turning over in his mind the prospect of inviting the Van Hoeks to Brockleston for the shooting in January. The last thing he wanted to do was to go back on his word, but he felt great trepidation at the prospect of them witnessing a fiasco similar to the ones that had occurred in recent weeks. His visit to the shoot that day was the final act in his making up his mind on the subject and he was now settled on his course of action. He would ring Frans Van Hoek that evening to extend his invitation to the family.

A light flurry of snow had started to fall and tiny light flakes drifted across the open doorway of the shoot shed as Victor opened it up for Hugo to leave. The keeper proffered two fine brace of pheasants to his lordship as he left, wishing him the compliments of the season.

"Thank you Drew, Mrs Lewis will do these proud I'm sure. While I think about it, if you've nothing on tomorrow can you pop up to the Hall in the afternoon for a chat? I've a few things to go over with you."

"Yes, very good sir." "Make it 4 o'clock, Victor, would you?"

"Will do, your lordship."

Hugo left the warmth of the shed, leaving the remaining revellers to finish off the vintage port, whisky and fruitcake that he had brought with him. Just after the door closed, Victor heard voices in the yard and a few seconds later the door opened again to reveal Nick Jones complete with a pair of walking sticks, struggling up the single step into the shed.

"Hi Vic, compliments of the season; thought I would look in even though I'm no use to anyone at the moment, let alone the beating line."

"Come on in Nick, we've had a decent day; sit yourself down here and have some of his lordship's good Scotch." PC Jones made himself at home in the closest available seat and Victor poured him a good tumbler of neat whisky.

"Steady on, Vic. I am nearly legless as it is." The two sat and talked for about an hour, by which time the shed had emptied and even the cooking pot had left on its journey back to the pub. Victor brought Nick up to date with all that had happened since his `accident` and Nick informed Victor about Harry Black's condition and his shortage of visitors. Victor felt a huge stab of guilt at the news; his efforts on the shoot had completely absorbed his thoughts over the last few weeks and he had almost forgotten about Harry.

"So he's likely to still be in at Christmas; I must see his wife and ask if she would like me to take her over there and if not go myself in any case." He thought it was the least he could do as he knew he was mainly responsible for the old man's condition.

"Talking of which, how are you getting back Nick? Surely you haven't driven here."

"No, Helen's dropped me off and I said I will ring when I want picking up; I had better do that now, thinking about it."

"Ring her now and ask her to pick you up at the cottage. We'll go back there for a cup of tea; it's damned cold in here now." The snow had started to stick and was even building up in small drifts in the gateways as the two made their way along the Brockleston Road to Keeper's Cottage. The flakes were now much larger and the wipers on the Discovery struggled to keep the windscreen clear.

"It's looking pretty bleak; ring Helen again and say you're staying the night here; there's no point in two of you ending up injured, you would never cope." Nick instantly saw the common sense in Victor's suggestion despite the prospect of spending the night in a damp cottage and he made the second call to his wife. Victor had suggested Nick staying for purely practical reasons, but the prospect of having some enjoyable company in the cottage for a change was very welcome.

After ushering Nick into the kitchen and sitting him down at the table, Victor sparked up the cooker and went outside for fresh logs. He was coated in fresh white snow when he returned.

"It's not easing up any, it's getting worse if anything; we may be cut off for a few hours in a bit; they don't plough and grit out here too soon; we are pretty low priority, being so far from the main roads." It wasn't long before Victor had bacon and eggs cooking in a large old cast iron frying pan and an assorted collection of bottles and cans of beer and lager sitting in the centre of the table to accompany the informal feast. There was no ceremony at Keeper's Cottage and Nick loved every minute of it, enjoying the company as much as Victor was. After consuming the rough and ready meal, the keeper reached across to the old dresser on the back wall of the kitchen and rummaged in a drawer before extracting a good-sized wooden cigar box

"Present from the shoot last Christmas, fancy one?"

"Why not," smiled Nick. They each selected one of the fat round Coronas and Victor produced an old cigar cutter and a box of matches. Neither of them was what you would call a 'smoker' but they both had a liking for a fine cigar once in a while. They sat in silence for a while, the rich blue smoke swirling about them.

"I know what else we need." Victor pulled a half full bottle of brandy out of the bottom cupboard of the dresser and furnished them both with half a tumbler full.

"How long have you been coming to the shoot Nick?"

"Thirteen years this time around Vic."

"More than most of the members, time doesn't half pass quickly as you get older." The two chatted on about the various shoot members and beaters past and present, going through another pair of cigars and a couple of further brandies each. Victor started upstairs to check the spare room, then realised that Nick would probably prefer downstairs rather than face the climb. Nick agreed and Victor made a bed up on the couch in the lounge.

"I'm just going to put my nose outside and see what the snow's doing." Victor went to the cottage door and peered out into the night. The snow had stopped falling and there was the distinctive sound of water dripping from the roof; it was thawing and unless there was a frost before morning the deep shroud of white that enveloped the village and fields would be almost gone by daybreak. Victor went back inside and sat back down.

"I will leave it an hour then have a drive round I think; the roads will be pretty accessible again by then I believe and as I hoped we won't be cut off from Limcester overnight."

The keeper helped his guest to the couch and settled him in before heading off to check the drives; the snow was melting quickly and the roads were now passable with care. There had been very few vehicles passing through since the start of the snowfall; even the pub had closed early; so it was fairly easy to spot if anything had stopped by a gateway or left the hard road into the fields. Victor did a full tour of the shoot even so; he still did not feel like leaving anything to chance despite the recent good spell. As it was he saw nothing but a couple of barn owls throughout his patrol and was back at home by around 4.30am. He crept into the cottage so as not to disturb the `sleeping policeman` in the lounge and made his way to bed where he managed to sleep until 8am before he was disturbed by Nick trying to feed logs into the cooker.

"Hey I'll get that; sorry you must have ended up cold, it dies down in the early hours as it is and I forgot to stoke it up last night." Victor stirred up the old cooker's heart and fed it with fuel then filled the electric kettle to make coffee; it would be some time before the old stove was hot enough to boil water.

"I'll run you back home in a bit Nick if that's ok."

"Fine, whenever you're ready, I've no rush to get anywhere." After a quick breakfast the two were on the road and Nick was soon back at home, his two Labradors going mad at seeing him again after yet another absence. By the time Victor got back to the outskirts of the village the last semblance of snow had disappeared and it was raining heavily, the combination of the melt water and the downpour transforming the already wet fields into sodden flats and the gateways and tracks into mud baths. John and Arthur would be having a pretty miserable Sunday out on the drives, he thought to himself as he neared home.

At 3.55pm the old Discovery arrived at Brockleston Hall; Victor parked it around the side near to the servants' entrance and walked to the front of the hall. He was highly conscious of how the old Land Rover loved to drop great clumps of mud from its wheel arches wherever it was parked at that time of year; and the embarrassment of that on the neatly raked chippings he could do without. The door was answered by Hugo himself, to Victor's surprise, and Lord Brockleston took him straight to the kitchen, where he seated him at the old pine table.

"I've given Reynolds and Lewis the day off Victor; thought they well deserved it." Hugo poured tea for them both from a huge teapot and pointed to a large plate of sandwiches sitting between them – "Do help yourself Drew. As you have probably heard I have invited some South Africans to stay in January and attend the shoot on a couple of Saturdays. I spoke to the Van Hoeks yesterday and they have accepted; they will be here for the first shoot after New Year." Hugo went on to tell Victor about the big game hunting and his time at Verwond Voet.

"So do you think our troubles have gone away, or should we still be on our guard?"

"There's no way to really tell sir, but I would say we should be watching out; it could be just the holiday season or something that's caused the break we've had."

"In that case I want you to have two more chaps to help out from now until after the visit; I will get Mowbray onto it tomorrow. I'm not having this lot get the better of us now I have guests coming." Jane walked into the kitchen and sat down.

"Daddy says he's down this way again tomorrow on some sort of business, says he might visit tomorrow afternoon. Should I invite him to dinner Hugo?"

"Yes, why not? It's a good old journey and no doubt he could do with breaking it up; no doubt he will stay the night." Victor thanked his host for the tea and the promise of yet more help and took his leave.

As Victor pulled onto Hall Lane to head back into the village he came across John Wrench walking home. John was soaked and mud splattered and had obviously had a hard day in the woods and fields.

"Get in John, let me take you home." The estate worker did not argue, glad of a break from the downpour and the darkness. He had nothing to report apart from the birds having a hard time from the weather very much like himself.

"Have you spoken to Arthur today?" the keeper asked.

"Saw him around noon, similar story with him up to then Vic." Victor dropped John off at his house and then went on to Harry Black's home, where he spoke to Harry's wife. Harry was still in hospital and she had not seen him that week. She said that for some reason he said he wasn't that bothered about her not visiting but she thought he was just trying to ease the pressure on her.

"Well, would you like to see him tomorrow afternoon? We could surprise him if I ran you over there?" She did not need asking twice and he arranged to pick her up just after midday.

# Chapter Sixteen

**M**OWBRAY HADN'T BEEN AT HIS desk for more than five minutes before the phone rang that Monday morning. Hugo was certainly not going to let the grass grow under his feet where the shoot was concerned. The agent wanted to argue against the decision but knew better than to do so; the tone of his lordship's voice made it very clear that the subject was not up for debate.

"Yes Lord Hugo, I will take a couple of the men off logging work. That should do it; it's got a bit wet for working in the far woods in any case this last week." Hugo rang off, leaving Mowbray less than pleased with this new demand on his workforce; but he set about organising the reassignment straightaway. He rang Victor at the cottage, disturbing him from his bed just after the keeper had managed to get to sleep, having been out on the shoot up until 7.30am.

"Ah Drew, good news for you; I am putting Simon Evans and Roger McAlister at your disposal as of now. His lordship has requested it; make sure you make good use of them; you now nearly have more staff than I have." Victor thanked Mowbray for the new staff and asked if he could direct them to John and Arthur for the time being; they could pretty much cover all the area effectively now for most of the day. The keeper then went back to bed to try to get some well-earned rest before lunchtime.

Mowbray called the two woodsmen into the estate office by means of a phone call to their foreman, John Butcher. They made an imposing sight as they entered; years of hard work outdoors had built them into hard looking fit men. Simon Evans stood at 6'4" and although Roger McAlister was fairly short in comparison at 5'8", he made up for it in his stout powerful limbs, torso and neck. If they had been drinking in a bar somewhere there weren't too many that would have tangled with them for fun. The agent explained to them why they had been called for and directed John to find

Arthur Young in the area of The Long Gorse and Roger to report to John Wrench in The Hall Wood.

Victor managed to get out of bed again at 12.30pm, having grabbed just a few hours' sleep; he had a quick 'make do' lunch as he tidied himself up and dressed before leaving to pick up Harry's wife. A few minutes later he was at the Black residence; Ethel Black was ready and waiting and the door of the house opened as he approached it.

"Hello Victor, it's good of you to offer to take me; I'm sure he will appreciate a visit especially as it's Christmas Eve tomorrow." Ethel was loaded up with stuff, struggling to carry it all; Victor took one of the carrier bags off her and helped her to the Discovery. Mrs Black was a quietly spoken, pleasant lady, quite unlike the way Harry had described her. He couldn't imagine her falling out with anyone; but then again he had not spent the best part of the last 30 years married to her and wasn't really in a position to comment, he thought to himself, recalling some of his own past marital arguments. Ethel seemed pretty well informed about the shoot even though she had never attended it herself, her only contact being the preparation and cooking of the game that Harry brought home after a shoot day. They talked easily and the conversation flowed as they drove to Limcester. They arrived at Limcester General and made their way to the ward. Victor stopped at the entrance and told Ethel to go on ahead. This would allow Ethel and Harry to have a few minutes alone before he went in.

"Don't be daft Victor, we've been married far too long for that to be an issue; you come on in, don't you be hanging around out here." They entered the orthopaedic ward, greeted by the distinctive aroma of such places, the sort of smell that you associated with illness, old age and institutions.

"He's just down here on the right." Ethel strode off down the corridor between the bays of beds either side, Victor following with the carrier bags. A tall, well-dressed man approached them in the opposite direction and they stepped aside to let him pass; he thanked them brusquely and strode off, leaving the ward. He was obviously in a hurry; no doubt an overworked consultant judging by his manner and the quality of his clothes. They entered the bay where Harry lay in the last bed on the right by the window; he was busy pushing something into the locker at the side of the bed and did not notice their approach.

"Hello handsome, surprise visitors for you." Harry looked up, not so much surprised as startled if anything.

"Blimey, I wasn't expecting you Eth, why didn't you tell me you were coming?"

"Like I said, thought we would surprise you, it being nearly Christmas and all." The old man then gained his composure and smiled.

"Well it's lovely to see you and nice to see you too Vic, thanks for bringing her in."

"Least I could do Harry, sorry I've not been in before, but things have been a bit hectic these last few weeks." Ethel then proceeded to play Santa, producing a selection of nicely wrapped gifts, cards and odds and ends that make a stay in hospital that bit more bearable. She pulled out a half bottle of whisky from her handbag, "I know you're not supposed to, but I'm not seeing you go without a snifter at this time of the year." Ethel went to secrete the bottle in Harry's bedside locker but he stopped her and grabbed it, concealing it beneath his bed sheet.

"I will stow that somewhere later love, there's no room in there." She was taken aback by his sudden movement but made no comment.

"Any sign of a reprieve yet Harry?"

"I don't know Vic, looks like it might be at least the New Year; they say the bone's not stable and it's got a touch of infection." Victor's trip to the hospital was doing nothing to ease his feelings of guilt and this last statement only made things worse. He decided to change the subject and went on to tell Harry about what was happening in Brockleston and the forthcoming visit by the South Africans.

"Whose is this?" Ethel picked up a mobile phone that was on top of the bedside locker.

"Must be one of the doctors', we can't use them in here."

"Yes, they seem to be rushing about a lot in here, no wonder they leave stuff lying about," observed Victor. The allotted two hours of visiting flew past; old Harry was at least decent company and made interesting conversation. Victor went outside ten minutes before the 4pm deadline, to leave Harry and Ethel alone for a few minutes; it may be the last time they would see each other that side of Christmas he thought.

Traffic was heavy around the hospital when they left, as it always was on weekday afternoons around Limcester. They made slow progress out of the town and it was around 6pm by the time Victor dropped Ethel off back at her house. She invited him in for tea, but he declined as he wanted to check in with Arthur and John to see how the day had gone and organise his assistants for the next few weeks. He drove around to Arthur Young's house and caught the joiner as he was just walking up his own path to the door.

"Hi Arthur, how's it gone today?"

"Alright Victor, no sign of any bother, Mowbray's sent us some good reinforcements too, so looks like we are winning." They went inside the house and Arthur's wife made them some tea as they sat in the cosy little front room with Victor outlining his plans to Arthur.

"Now what I'm proposing is some 24 hour security cover over the next few weeks; just to get us through the period leading up to and during the visit by the South Africans. I know it's not a good time of year for any one of you because of Christmas; but it will probably be only for a fortnight at the most. If I leave myself out of the rota I can fill in when one of you needs a break and it leaves me to organise the shoot days and do the feeding." Arthur listened intently to what Victor was saying, expressing no surprise at what the keeper was saying; he had expected as much. Victor said he would leave it up to the four of them to decide on who was working at what time, but he wanted at least two of them around at any one time and the two sides of the shoot covering as before. Arthur proposed back to back twelve-hour shifts with changeovers at 7pm and 7am; Victor thought this a good idea.

"We will kick it off tomorrow morning after you've had a chance to talk it over with the others; I will cover tonight as usual; if there are any problems let me know and I'll have to re-think it." Victor left and headed for home, hoping to have a few hours' rest before his night patrol.

Victor took to the fields and woods of the shoot at around 11.30pm that night, starting off with a long walk through Solomon's Wood; he still had the feeling that it was the most vulnerable due to its outlying position and its previous devastation. As Christmas Eve started he was standing alone next to where the release pen had been, haunted by all those familiar memories and thoughts that always came to visit him at such times; ghosts of the past and even spectres of the present. His Father, Susan, Storm, Bill Flemming and even Harry Black – all walked with him for a short time as he stepped through the silence of the wood. Apart from the wildlife, these thoughts were his only company; his tormentors were again notable by their absence, to his relief. He returned to the Land Rover and continued on his journey across the shoot.

$$*\,*\,*\,*\,*$$

Across at Brockleston Hall, Hugo was entertaining his prospective father-in-law, playing billiards in the games room with Richard Rotherby-Hyde. `Limited Liability` had arrived in the early evening and enjoyed dinner with Hugo and Jane; he was now discussing business and investments with Hugo, and Jane had retired earlier, leaving the two alone.

"What you need Hugo is a nice little earner to prop things up for you; there's not much here at Brockleston that will provide a long term means of support to your lifestyle." Rotherby-Hyde went on to demean the prospects of future incomes from shooting, agriculture and forestry, selling Hugo the merits of investment and the underwriting world. Realising he had got Hugo's full attention he then came out with what he had been leading up to: "Jack Melton and I have come upon a cracking opportunity in Ecuadorian Oil, there's a new company venturing out into the rain forest just north of Coca. It's an established area; they've found some new ground and are just waiting on permission from the government to exploit it. What they're after are initial funds to oil the wheels with the authorities, so to speak. There's going to be some big fast profits for those in from the start." He went on to explain that `Nap Oil` wasn't listed on the stock market as it had not been floated yet and it was all being kept to a limited number of investors initially, hence the prospect of huge profits for a lucky few.

"So what do you say Hugo, worth a closer look?"

"Well yes, don't see why not. You and Jack are sound enough chaps to set out with; you've never gone hungry."

"We'll talk more tomorrow then old boy." The two wound up the game and made their way up the stairs to bed.

# Chapter Seventeen

THE LIGHTS ON THE BIG decorated tree that almost filled one corner of the bar in the 'Brockleston Arms' twinkled brightly across the room; Bill Stewart had dimmed the lights in the pub to show the tree to best effect. The blazing log fire completed the festive atmosphere and trade was swift as it always was on Christmas Eve. Folks from the Village who never usually set foot in the pub for the rest of the year were out in force. There had been a group out carol singing around the houses, making a collection for St John's, and even the rarely seen Vicar was amongst the group that were indulging in the hot sausage rolls and mince pies that Bill had laid on for them. Outside in the lane the scene was far from seasonal; the snow of a few days earlier was no more than a distant memory and the rough tarmac was being washed again by torrential rain which had held off just long enough to see the revellers into 'The Brocky'. Victor stood at the bar talking to the landlord and making use of the free hot fare. He was enjoying the opportunity of spending a few hours in the company of others instead of preparing for his usual nightly patrol of the last few weeks.

As the bells started to ring at St John's, calling the festive worshippers to the midnight mass, Roger McAlister was already five hours into his night vigil in The Hall Wood. The sound of the bells was just about audible to him, carried on the wind through the driving rain from the other side of the Brockleston Road. He had managed to find shelter in an old hut used to store bags of grain. The hut was close to one of the old release pens, making it a convenient storage site for pheasant food and a handy shelter for any keeper working at the pen. Roger sat on an upturned wooden beer crate, rolling himself a cigarette and wondering if he would manage to stay awake all night. As it turned out he had no reason to worry on that front. As he was about to light his roll-up he heard the sound of voices from the direction of the nearby ride. He placed the unlit cigarette in his tobacco tin and returned it to his coat pocket. He pulled the shed door shut and listened; the voices were getting louder, they were heading his way. He tried to look through a small gap in the rotting wooden boards but could see nothing but the darkness of the night. Within a few minutes he could tell that whoever it was out there was passing the hut just a few yards from him.

"Why did the silly old sod have to fall in there, that's what I want to know? Walking around those woods in the middle of the night at his age; should know bloody better, bloody pain in the arse now not knowing what's going on round here." Roger caught part of the conversation as they passed. He waited a few seconds for the two to pass before slowly exiting the hut and following at a discreet distance, just concealed by the darkness. He could just make out that one of them was carrying a sack, which appeared to be heavy by the way he was stooping. They headed for one of the nearby feeders and one of them lifted the lid while the other appeared to get ready to pour the contents of the sack into it. Just as their attention was taken up with the task in hand Roger made ground on them and swung the stout stick he was carrying. The heavy end of the piece of hawthorn made contact with Hatton's skull as he bent over the hopper with the sack. The lights went out for Elvis and the king left the stage, slumping into immediate unconsciousness as the hard wood embedded itself in his dura mater having fractured his skull like a thin eggshell, such was the force of the blow from the stout woodsman, fuelled by the adrenaline of raw fear. The sack fell to the floor of the wood, scattering its contents as it went. Hampton took a few seconds to connect with reality, taken by complete surprise, staring in disbelief at the motionless form of his erstwhile partner. He reacted like a cornered fox. Lashing out at whatever had attacked them, he rained frenzied kicks and punches at the shadowy figure that loomed before him. His right fist connected with the orbit of Roger's left eye, knocking the woodsman back in a dazed state before he turned and ran like a frightened hare. Roger got to his feet and ran after Hampton through the darkness, tripping and stumbling over the clinging briars as he went. He could make no ground on his quarry; the wiry Hampton ran like his sort always did, fast, the habit of a lifetime's running from the law. Despite the short time of the pursuit the woodsman had got some distance by the time he gave up and headed back towards the wounded Hatton. It took him several minutes to walk back to the feed hopper. When he got back to where it had started all that remained was the half-empty sack, his hawthorn stick and scattered grains; there was no sign of Hatton. He leaned back and sighed; he didn't know if he was more relieved to see that he had not killed the man or frustrated that he had got away; either way he supposed it made life simpler, he thought. He shone his torch around the area; the grains of wheat lying around appeared to be coated with some sort of white powder; it could just have been wheat flour from broken grains but he doubted it. He had grown up in the countryside and had been a farm worker on the estate when required so he knew what whole wheat grains usually looked like. If the white powder was poison it would explain why the two had been trying to fill a hopper in the middle of the night; helping out with pheasant feeding was not really their style. He put on his work gloves and scooped up the spilled grain into the sack, lifting the leaf litter with it in an attempt to get all of it out of harm's way. Having satisfied himself that he had cleared most of the grain, he picked up the sack and walked back to the hut. He sat back down on the beer crate and picked up a piece of baler twine from the floor. He wrapped this around the neck of the sack and tied it securely. He then placed the suspect sack just outside the door of the hut to avoid it getting mixed up with the other sacks already in the hut. Taking out his tobacco tin he opened it and took out the cigarette he had rolled before the disturbance. He leaned back on the grain sacks behind him, enjoying the calming effect of the familiar Virginia tobacco. A few minutes later the woodsman started to feel nauseous, a few seconds after that he was convulsing on the dusty floor of the hut, retching and vomiting and struggling for breath, a few seconds after that he was dead.

Hatton was still dazed as he ran up the ride in the direction of the hall. He didn't know where he was heading; he only knew that Hampton had abandoned him. His instinct was to put as much distance between him and the scene of his crimes as he could and this drove him on. The intense throbbing pain in the back of his head took second place to his flight as a sticky mix of blood and cerebrospinal fluid oozed down onto his shirt collar. As he reached the clump of three oaks he too started to feel sick and he stopped to lean against one of the ancient tree trunks. His legs buckled and darkness overtook him, easing his panic and pain. Half an hour later the massive swelling that developed within his skull closed down its blood supply and the king was dead.

Hampton made it back to where they had hidden their latest vehicle, an old black Ford Escort; they had parked it just behind a hedge on the Limcester side of Keeper's Cottage. He started up the protesting engine and sped off towards his unkempt earth in the town caring only for his own welfare. He knew Hatton was as resourceful as he was and that even if he was picked up, he would be saying nothing to the police and if he had died, well, the same rules would still apply.

Victor came out of St John's at just after 12.45am; he had enjoyed the service and meeting up with people he had not spoken to in some time. David Radford had taken him down to the church in his Range Rover and was now taking him back to the cottage, both totally unaware of the drama that had unfolded and the two bodies that now lay close by, cooling in the damp cold air of Christmas Day. The keeper was in bed just after 1am, still oblivious to recent events.

# Chapter Eighteen

Arthur Young and John Wrench met up at the estate yard at just before 7am on Christmas Day morning. Apart from the sound of tractors working in the yards of nearby stock and dairy farms all was silent in Brockleston. The engines of the tractors seemed that bit louder than usual as stockmen hurried with their usual routines of feeding, mucking out and bedding down; keen to get home early to enjoy time with their families before having to return to repeat the whole process in the late afternoon. Simon Evans arrived from his night vigil soon after.

"How's it gone Simon, anything to report?"

"No all pretty quiet, heard nothing all night apart from the church bells."

"Heard anything of Roger?"

"No, not a thing; I hope he hasn't been asleep; he's bad enough in the daytime when he gets in the woods." They waited for 20 minutes but there was still no sign of Roger.

"Well, John and I had better get off to the woods; we might find him there. Could you nip round to his house and see if he's gone home to see his kids before you knock off Simon?" They went their separate ways, Simon heading into the village and calling at Roger McAlister's house, where a bleary eyed wife said she had not seen him since 6.30pm the night before.

"Why, what's up, where is he?"

"Probably asleep somewhere, he'll be home in a bit." Simon left the woman worrying with her two children, who were still waiting until dad came home to see them open their presents.

John Wrench headed straight to the top end of The Hall Wood; he intended to make a search through the wood back towards Home Farm. A few minutes later he was running back to the estate yard. He had cut through the three oaks and found something he had not liked the look of; it was face down and cold with a big wound on the back of its head; but he knew whatever it was it was not Roger. The yard was empty as he fumbled for his keys to open up the joiner's shop to use the phone. A few seconds later Victor picked up the receiver at Keeper's Cottage and the alarm was raised.

Within the hour police had sealed off the entire area to the south east of the Brockleston Road. Brockleston Hall, The Hall Wood, Home Farm and the Estate Yard were all being treated as a crime scene. Christmas Day was going to be very expensive for the Constabulary. Victor and his three remaining assistants were all gathered at the hall along with Hugo and Jane. DCI Lewis was using the coach house at the Hall as a temporary incident room. He had already got his home comforts sorted out; a large bottled gas powered space heater was holding back the December cold and a radio link had been set up. The first officers at the scene had already identified Elvis Hatton; they were traffic patrolmen from Limcester, colleagues of Nick Jones. There was no doubt who the unloved long term miscreant was. The rest of the unanswered questions were not as easy to address. The mustering of officers and setting in place of all the machinery necessary for a murder investigation were hampered by the outlying location and the fact that it was Christmas Day. Bob Lewis was not in the best of moods. As on call senior detective cover over the festive period he just expected to give a bit of advice over the phone in between enjoying the celebrations with his family; standing in an old coach house having to think under pressure was not how he had planned things. He was further aggravated by the discovery of who the victim was and the amount of money that would have to come out of his budget as a matter of course to investigate his death. It was early afternoon by the time the first police search team started a sweep of The Hall Wood and it wasn't before 3pm that the unfortunate Roger McAlister's body was found in the little hut. Roger's wife was already frantic with worry; the arrival of all the police in the village had helped fuel her anxiety as the day wore on and she had been ringing all morning for information. The message that it was not Roger that had been found amongst the three oaks gave temporary hope; until a family liaison officer and detective sergeant went to the house to inform her about Roger's discovery. Victor had volunteered to go up to the scene and identified what lay in his storage hut as his short lived assistant. Tents were erected over the bodies where they lay, lighting equipment brought in and inner cordons set up. The circus had greatly increased in size and complexity by early evening when a Home Office Pathologist attended and carried out his initial examinations before the bodies could finally be removed under escort to Limcester. A home-coming for Hatton, a sad departure for Roger McAlister, as his widow and children watched the convoy of hearse and police car head out of the village down the Brockleston Road. A Christmas they would never forget and a scar that would mark their minds for the rest of their lives.

The investigation proceeded steadily over the following days; the entire Brockleston Estate Staff were interviewed along with enquiries involving nearly all of the residents. Despite the lengthy questioning of Victor, Arthur, John and Simon, very little information was released to them regarding what had been found. Victor revealed everything that he knew, apart from the episode involving the preparing of the pit in Graves Spinney; he did not want to knowingly hamper any enquiry into Roger's death. He was devastated enough about it as it was. It was the day after New Year's Day before the outer cordon was lifted and life at the Hall and estate yard started to resume with subdued normality. The area around the three oaks and the top end of The Hall Wood remained closed off and guarded by some very cold, wet and bored police officers.

Hampton was picked up shortly after Hatton's body was identified, but despite encouragement and threats from Bob Lewis himself in hours of protracted interviewing, he was telling them nothing of any use. It was no use trying to forensically link the two as it was common knowledge they had lived and run together for years and any sharing of fibres, DNA, or other evidence was pretty inconsequential. However the heat was turned up when clothing and footwear from the flat was found to be contaminated with soil and vegetation similar to that found in The Hall Wood; but it was that word `similar` that Hatton and his solicitor picked up on. There was no hard evidence without Hatton's account and that wasn't forthcoming, nor was it likely to be. The only other people that could say with any certainty what had occurred in the wood that Christmas Eve were now far beyond being able to comment.

The forensic team were able to link Roger and Hatton due to blood and tissue fragments found on the stick and Roger's clothing; unusually there had been no contamination of Hampton by the blood spatter from Elvis's head, and he had been wearing gloves when he punched Roger's eye.

The subsequent Home Office post mortem examinations and related analytical work revealed that the wound to Hatton's skull had resulted in a fatal brain compression developing and that Roger had died as a result of strychnine poisoning; the toxin likely to have been absorbed via his last cigarette. A number of dead pheasants found in the vicinity of a feeder not too far from the one where the fight had occurred were also found to have ingested the poison. The picture was becoming pretty clear by now and DCI Lewis was under pressure to 'wrap things up' at Brockleston as the second week of the New Year started. The scene was cleared up and the bodies released, leaving a reduced team of detectives to clear up the loose ends and prepare the reports for the coroner. For the time being nothing could be done with Hatton, and Roger and Elvis were both equally killer and victim in their own right as things stood.

Nearly all of Brockleston attended at St John's for Roger's funeral service. Lord Brockleston had organised it in consultation with his devastated wife and funded it in its entirety. As Victor stood at the graveside listening to the final words said over Roger, he glanced across at another all too recently disturbed mass of soil. Fresh flowers adorned the little patch of earth where Harry Black had taken up residency a few days earlier. The old lad had developed a chest infection, which had turned to pneumonia, and he had gone the way that many his age did after sustaining a badly broken bone. Harry was now dressed better than he had ever been in life – wearing the funeral director's top of the range coffin, paid for in cash with the haul of money his wife had found in his bedside locker when she cleared it out after she had said her last goodbye to her husband in that dull ward so far from home. Ethel never mentioned the contents of the buff envelope to anyone but guessed that it had been connected to the goings on around the shoot and Harry's sudden interest in going out for walks late at night.

Nicholas Gordon

As he walked out of the church gates the Brockleston keeper found himself wondering if maintaining his livelihood and a bit of traditional sport was really worth all the misery it had brought into the lives of himself and those around him. Just at that moment he felt the responsibility resting firmly on his own shoulders; not those of Lord Brockleston, Mowbray, the shoot members or any animal rights activists or criminals that might be behind it all.

# Chapter Nineteen

**A**FTER A THOROUGH CLEAR UP in The Hall Wood, removing all the feeders and grain to ensure there was no further contamination, the shoot was again ready for business for the last Saturday in January, traditionally the beaters' shoot. After allowing John, Arthur and Simon time to help Victor with the clean-up and subsequent checking for any further poisoned birds or wildlife, Mowbray returned them all to their normal duties. Hugo had felt obliged to reimburse the shoot with part of its rent and Mowbray had argued that all the additional costs incurred by the recent upheaval needed to be addressed in some way. Hugo had lost his enthusiasm for maintaining the shooting at all cost. The price paid by Roger McAlister for protecting the game at Brockleston was far too high to contemplate. The three estate workers were only too pleased to be sent back to their normal duties; their time on the shoot had not turned out to be a happy one; Simon was probably the worst affected, having to return to the logging operation without his old friend.

Hugo had been put in the embarrassing position of having to contact the Van Hoeks and apologise to them for having to put off their visit to Brockleston. With the re-opening of the shoot for the final day he was contemplating asking them over to participate in the beaters' day; common decency dictated that he should consult with Victor and Robbie Langdon over this even though he would have had the final say in any case. He invited the two over to the Hall on the last Monday in January. The captain and keeper sat in the drawing room as Hugo explained his situation and asked what they thought of him inviting the South Africans to shoot on the day reserved as recognition for all the hard work of the beaters over the season. Robbie turned to Victor.

"Well Vic, it's really up to you traditionally, it's your day and you get to invite who you like."

"Well I have no problem with it, your lordship, and sadly we are well down on shooters for the day in any case due to recent events. It would be nice to have a decent day to mark the end of the season after all that's happened."

"Thanks, you've helped me out of a spot chaps; I will ring them directly and see if I can't rectify the situation."

***** 

Frans Van Hoek's deep accent answered when Hugo called him that evening.

"Ah Lord Hugo, nice to hear from you; how is everything now, has the dust settled over there yet?" Hugo told Frans about how the situation had turned out and apologised for the short notice before asking him to Saturday's shoot.

"We would be delighted to attend; the boys have been miserable since you last rang cancelling things. I will see if we can get a flight, that's the only thing that might stop us. Will get back to you either way and thank you again your lordship."

The South Africans landed at Heathrow at midday on Friday and by the evening, the three darkly tanned faces of Frans, Pieter and Johan were around the dining table at Brockleston Hall sampling some of Annie Lewis's best culinary creations. Anna had not travelled with them and had remained at Verwond Voet to hold the fort in their absence.

"He looks well up there; strange to see something from home hanging up there like that in the middle of England though," Frans Van Hoek laughed and pointed to the huge mounted head of the Wildebeest that hung at the end of the room.

"Yes, they did a good job on him I'm pleased to say; would have been a real crime if they hadn't with that magnificent beast." The conversation naturally turned to shooting. By the time Jim Reynolds was passing round the table with the cigars and brandy, the three visitors were highly excited at the prospect of their first taste of English driven game. Hugo explained that it was the end of the season and things may not be as good as they might have

144

been prior to Christmas, but this did nothing to dampen their enthusiasm.

Saturday morning saw Robbie Langdon, Mowbray and Victor at the shoot shed early. They were planning to pull off a good day for Lord Hugo's guests. Robbie and Victor were motivated by the desire to preserve the shoot as usual; the agent motivated to continue on the right side of Hugo. It was usually the case on beaters' day that Victor would use every drive on the shoot in an attempt to provide some sport. So the planning wasn't too difficult in terms of which drives were going to be used. It just remained to decide in what order they would be shot in order to keep the birds that were disturbed and missed 'in play', minimising those that went out of the shoot area or into woods that had already been driven. It was quickly decided to start at Solomon's Wood, driving the birds towards Brockleston; then proceed on to the other three drives in turn back towards the road. Graves Spinney would be the first drive after lunch at the 'Brockleston Arms'; and then across to the drives at Brockleston Pits and The Hall Wood. It was planned to keep the birds shot from The Hall Wood separate and dispose of them safely, just in case there were still any carrying traces of strychnine although this was now highly unlikely.

The Van Hoeks were up early; their enthusiasm of the previous evening had not diminished as they helped themselves to the mounds of sausages, bacon, eggs, kedgeree and toast laid out on the sideboard of the dining room. Hugo had directed Mrs Lewis to put on a good spread throughout their visit and his instructions had not gone unheeded. After they had been thoroughly sated Hugo and Jim Reynolds took them to the gun room to fix them up with shotguns for the day. Pieter and Johan could hardly contain their excitement at being in such a traditional looking gun room. After much mounting to their shoulders of various 12 bores by all three of the South Africans they finally decided on the weapons that they were most comfortable with. Reynolds then placed the chosen guns into leather gun slips, labelling each with the name of its intended user before he took them outside to the car and proceeded to fill cartridge bags for them all.

By the time Lord Hugo and his guests arrived at Home Farm, the rest of the party had already assembled in the shoot shed. Eager beaters were collecting their shoot cards from Robbie Langdon and the regular guns were drinking coffee from their flasks before setting off on their day as beaters. David Radford was not present as he had gone abroad on holiday and Phillip Boddington was organising the sweep in his place. All went quiet as Lord Hugo and the Van Hoeks entered the shed; Mowbray was first to greet them followed by Robbie Langdon and Victor; then they were circulated around the other guns and interspersed beaters.

Robbie Langdon then called the group to order and made his short speech, welcoming Lord Hugo and his guests and paying respects to Roger McAlister before moving onto the usual shoot briefing.

A short time later the group moved off, heading to Solomon's Wood. As they turned out of Hall Lane and headed left along the Brockleston Road, Victor saw three minibuses approaching the village from the direction of Limcester but thought nothing of it. Probably a group of walkers that were going to meet at the pub and perhaps do the usual tour of the footpaths, the keeper thought to himself. When they arrived at the far wood Robbie Langdon marshalled his beating team to the far side of the wood whilst Victor organised his guns for the day. Despite the break with tradition he made sure the three special guests were placed in good spots, tweaking their positions in the line to get them standing in what he thought were the better positions. When Victor blew the whistle to start the drive off Robbie moved into the wood with the beating line and they walked slowly towards the guns. The first pheasant appeared over the tops of the trees, flying straight and high over the waiting guns, helped by the ground falling away towards the Long Gorse beneath them. The shooting started and the guns gave a good account of themselves, the three South Africans especially so. They were well practised in shooting difficult birds flushed out of scrub and the nicely presented high pheasants were giving them no problems at all. The dogs were kept well-employed picking up all the shot birds and their handlers were having an equally enjoyable time. When Robbie Langdon blew the horn to mark the end of the drive the assembled guns broke their weapons and unloaded, most of them well satisfied with how the day was going.

The enforced break from shooting at Brockleston appeared to have allowed the game to settle back in and concentrate in the original woods again.

The group then went on to The Long Gorse to try to repeat the performance. The guns lined out along the wide southern side of the wood with their backs to Old Jack's Slang and waited for the whistle to blow and the beaters to move off again. Just after the whistle sounded Andrew Probert heard a voice just behind him and turned to look. He was faced with an untidy column of people filing through the gap between the two halves of the Slang. They were carrying banners and some of them had air horns which they started sounding as others commenced shouting at the guns.

"MEET THE ANIMAL DEFENDERS!"
"STOP THE SLAUGHTER!"
"NO MORE KILLING AT BROCKLESTON!"

and various other anti-shooting slogans were shouted amongst the loud penetrating blasts from the horns. The same slogans were scrawled in bold red letters across the banners that were being carried. There must have been at least 40 protestors. Victor saw that the three minibuses he had seen earlier were parked on the Brockleston Road close to Lady Jane's Moss. Mowbray, who was standing with Hugo, was on his mobile phone already, contacting the police. Victor shouted

"Nobody shoot yet" and blew his whistle trying to attract Robbie Langdon's attention in the wood. The protestors lined out in front of the guns to prevent any shooting and continued their chanting and yelling, waving their placards and banners as they did so.

"Where the hell have this lot come from Victor?" Hugo shouted across to the keeper.

"I don't know your Lordship; I've not seen the like of it before, not around here anyway." It was obvious that the group were going to stay for as long as it took. The guns were broken and unloaded and Robbie and his beating members emerged from the back of the wood and came to join them.

"Bloody hell Vic, what's going on, this has put the mockers on the day hasn't it?" The captain made his way over to where Hugo, Mowbray and the Van Hoeks had gathered.

147

"A fine mess again Robbie, different flavour to usual, but a fine mess just the same."

"Yes, Lord Hugo, today of all days too; has anyone rung the police?"

"Yes, they said they shouldn't be long, there's some still in the area doing enquiries they said." About five minutes later two figures were seen walking towards the shoot. It took them some time to get across the fields; they were two detectives in their city shoes and they were not best pleased to have been sent on such an errand, but uniform patrols were still a good distance off.

"DS Phillips, Sir, what's happened?" The first of the two officers introduced himself to Robbie as the captain had walked away from the group and met them just as they emerged from the outskirts of the Slang.

"This lot have just turned up out of the blue and disrupted everything as you can see; can you do anything about it Officer?"

"I'll see what's going on and ask them to leave; I shouldn't imagine they will take much notice of me though." The two officers went over to the protestors and spoke with some of them. There didn't appear to be any sort of leader with the group, but they all said they were there to stop the shoot and that they wouldn't be dissuaded from their purpose. Some of the shooters started to lose their cool, angry that their one day of sport for the season had been disrupted. The two officers went to them and warned them about their conduct and started taking names. This did nothing to help the situation and Hugo went to them to voice his opinion.

"Look here, these are my guests on my land; that crowd over there are trespassing and interfering with what is still a legal activity. We called you to get rid of them, where are the rest of you, a couple of weeks ago you couldn't move around here for you lot." The Sergeant then took exception to his lordship and also warned him about his behaviour. At that moment four uniformed officers arrived accompanied by DCI Lewis. Lewis went straight to Hugo and asked what the problem was; Lord Brockleston had no hesitation in telling him.

"Look here Sir, your shoot has already taken up far too much of mine and the constabulary's time for this year and last year as well, come to think of it. I am now telling you to end your sporting activities for the day or I will be taking people in to prevent a breach of the peace and I don't much care on which side of this argument

148

they are sitting."

"Well, thank you very much for your help Officer, it's nice to see my taxes are well spent; now please take your men and get off my property; if you can't help then please don't hinder." Hugo turned his back on Lewis and took his guests back to the vehicles. They headed back to the road accompanied by the rest of the shoot.

"What's wrong with this country Hugo? I can't believe what I've just seen; your police are a damned disgrace."

"I know Frans, it's the way it's going; I have been told about such things but not witnessed it for myself until today."

The shoot retired to 'The Brockleston Arms'; the whole mood of the group was sour and subdued. They parked the vehicles along the road outside the pub's front windows at Victor's suggestion, so that they could be watched from the pub windows to prevent any sabotage being done to them. The three minibuses had followed on after them and were all parked up close by, their occupants watching the guns and beaters enter the pub. Hugo invited all present to take a drink with him then went and sat at a table close to the fire with his guests and Mowbray.

"Bloody Hell!" he said then fell silent. The fact that he had dragged three valued acquaintances half way across the globe on the pretence of a good day's shooting only to witness what had just occurred consumed his every thought. He started to apologise, but it felt futile and insincere.

"Not to worry Hugo, it was good whilst it lasted; it's a shame that those buggers are so well protected over here or we could have had a nice addition to the day's sport." Hugo looked up and laughed.

"Yes I do wonder which one of us lives in the civilised country nowadays Frans, I really do."

An early lunch was served at the pub a short time later and the group continued drinking up to around 3pm, when people started to drift off out of the pub. Lord Brockleston and his party left after thanking an embarrassed Victor for his efforts during the past season. By 4pm only Victor and Robbie Langdon remained, sitting on high stools at the bar.

"Any ideas where that lot came from Vic?"

"None whatsoever, all pretty young and pretty disorganised,

but they soon had the better of us thanks to Lewis and his incompetents; Nick told me it was him that refused to help us out months ago when Storm was killed."

"Makes you wonder where we're living, doesn't it?" The two stayed for another half hour before Robbie got up and announced that he was leaving.

"Well Vic that's it for another season; shame it ended on such a bad note, but that's been the pattern this year; don't know what'll happen next time round; a lot of the guns are pretty fed up with it all. Anyway see you soon and we'll see what happens next." The captain said goodbye to Bill Stewart and was gone out of the door. Victor followed soon after. He climbed into the old Discovery and drove slowly back to the cottage. He felt that things did not really have much purpose just at that moment and he was heading home just because there was nowhere else to go.

The Students' Union Bar at Limcester College was particularly busy that evening; a large group of students seemed to have money to throw around and they were making full use of it; many of them drunk to the point of vomiting by 8pm. Their anonymous animal welfare minded benefactor had been very generous with his cash payment that they found under their seats in the minibuses that had picked them up that morning for their trip to Brockleston.

# Chapter Twenty

THE VAN HOEKS STAYED AT Brockleston Hall for two days following the disastrous shoot day, with Hugo and Jane desperately trying to play the good hosts. But there was only so much that could be found to keep them amused in Brockleston and the nearby area. The end of the shooting season was always marked by a bit of a slack period in the calendar for those that didn't also follow or ride to hounds and the weather was nearly always uninspiring at that time of year.

Hugo decided on his next course of action; they would all go to London and spend some time there. There was plenty to show the Van Hoeks in the capital, not least a brief visit to where the excellent Wildebeest trophy had been mounted; Hugo knew this would particularly appeal to Frans. The South Africans thought the London trip was a great idea and the following morning they all left Limcester station together bound for the capital. Hugo felt that he could at least salvage something of his dignity by showing his guests a good time in London and his mood was much better as they all relaxed in the business class seats on the train. The group then spent three days together seeing the sights, taking in West End shows and enjoying the very best meals before Hugo escorted Frans and his sons to Heathrow for their return flight. The rough spoken Frans gave Hugo a rib-crushing hug and shook his hand with extreme violence before he left for the departure lounge; the South African had truly enjoyed his stay despite the problems; he wasn't a man to wrap up or hide his feelings, that wasn't his way. The two brothers also shook hands firmly with Hugo and they all parted as good friends.

Hugo and Jane then went on to stay at the Rotherby-Hydes; Jane's mother had insisted on it as soon as she heard they were in

London. She had seen very little of her daughter since the couple had returned to England and so they felt obliged to accept. Hugo had grown tired of Brockleston again; the initial pleasure he had felt on his return home had long since faded. The torrid catalogue of events since his arrival there, culminating in the death of Roger McAlister; then the severe anti-climax of the beaters' shoot had done nothing to enamour him of his place of birth. Now its much-needed financial stability was also threatened and he no longer viewed it as his golden goose; the bird was ill and he did not know what to do with it. It was in this frame of mind that Hugo found himself during his next lengthy conversation with Richard Rotherby-Hyde in his study after dinner the following evening. Rotherby-Hyde leaned back in his leather office chair, brandy glass in hand.

"Thought any more about Ecuador, Hugo? Need to move on pretty sharpish now the market's turning again you know."

"I don't know, with the way things are at Brockleston right now, I may need any spare money I have to prop things up, don't know if I want to take a gamble with it."

"Well the offer's still there, but don't take forever and it's a gamble with a very small `g` believe me, or I wouldn't be looking at it." The conversation continued along these lines for several minutes, Rotherby-Hyde sounding more like a cheap sales man than a prospective father-in-law.

"Tell you what, old man, why don't you take a trip out there next week with me and see the set up for yourself. No harm in looking is there and a stint abroad might take your mind off recent events."

"Alright, sounds fine, I was thinking of going back to the Bahamas soon anyway; we might as well go via Ecuador."

The following Tuesday afternoon Hugo, Jane and her father boarded a KLM flight from Schipol to Quito via Bonaire in the Dutch Antilles, on the first leg of their long haul journey to the Amazon rain forest. The cold air caused them all to shiver as they left the warmth of the terminal building for the short walk along the covered gangway to the aircraft. It had already gone dark and the temperature had plummeted with the setting of the sun. The highly efficient Dutch cabin crew welcomed them aboard and showed them to their seats, where they settled in for the fourteen hour first leg. Hugo felt as if it was only the week before that he had flown into Heathrow from his hunting trip to South Africa as he settled into his comfortable upper class seat. What was it about the isolation from the rest of the world that long haul flights did to the mind he thought? It was as if life was on hold for some interminable time as you were transported across the globe in a big metal tube with wings, accompanied only by the incessant drone of the engines that could never be escaped no matter how hard you tried to block it out. Travelling at unimaginably high speeds, but seeming to be crawling along as the vastness of the world stretched below, rendering everything into insignificance. He knew that the events of the last few weeks would come to visit him again on the flight, along with his financial worries. He hoped Rotherby-Hyde would not be too intense; if he was there was really no way of escape from his prospective father-in-law and now co-investor. Jane smiled across at him as she fastened her seatbelt and prepared for the take-off; her father was engrossed in the *Financial Times*, for the moment oblivious to everything around him. A short time later they were heading back the way they had flown into Holland from Heathrow. The lights of the dykes and roads twinkled beneath them in the freezing air, looking like stale reminders of the recently passed festive period. They flew down across the English coast then on to the vastness of the Atlantic, over which the bulk of the journey would be spent.

"Been to South America before Hugo?"

"Yes, I've been to Panama and Cuba, and had a good tour of Brazil a couple of years ago, but never ventured to Ecuador."

"Quito's a funny old place, plays hell with my breathing at times; it's like there's no air, especially late at night. We won't be there for long though, just one night before flying on to Coca and then going up the Napo to where the proposed site is." Hugo was relieved that apart from this brief conversation over their in-flight dinner, his father-in-law said very little on the flight. Even he found it hard to talk on an aircraft it appeared. The only advantage to taking several long haul flights in close proximity to each other, was that the familiarity with the conditions aboard the plane made it easier to relax and shortly after the meal all three had reclined their seats and fallen asleep.

In the early hours of the morning the Captain announced that they would soon be landing in the Caribbean. The jet made a smooth descent onto the Dutch tarmac of Bonaire airport and it was then announced that passengers could disembark to the small terminal building whilst the plane was refuelled, re-stocked and cleaned. Hugo and Jane took advantage of the welcome opportunity to stretch their legs and briefly enter the outside world again. Richard Rotherby-Hyde remained on board; he said the airport held no attraction for him as he had passed through a few times before and was quite comfortable where he was. The fresh, almost fragrant, hot tropical breeze hit them as they descended the steps to the tarmac. It was like some strange dream in the middle of the night, the spell only broken by the airport officials herding them along and hurrying them along the marked route to the terminal. At the entrance they were sorted into arrival and transit passengers, Hugo and Jane being given yellow passes as they entered the building. Inside it was cool and fresh, good air conditioning maintained a comfortable temperature, potted palms and a cosy looking bar across the back wall completed the effect. On the right hand side of the building there were some small but very well-stocked shops selling duty free alcohol, tobacco, perfume and jewellery. After a brief tour of the sales' outlets, they sat in the cool air of the lounge enjoying the break from the aero engines. Just under an hour later they were asked to return to the plane and made the short walk back to the jet, again shepherded by the throng of airport staff.

Just after take off the captain announced that the next leg of the journey would take them to Guayaquil near the Pacific Coast and then onto Quito in the Andes.

"Not another landing and stop off, surely?" Hugo remarked, as much to himself as anything.

"Yes, sorry, forgot to mention that; this plane becomes a bit of a local shuttle when it gets this side of the Atlantic," Jane's father replied to Hugo. The short break at Bonaire had unsettled his lordship and he found it hard to get back into the mind set for travelling again; the thought of many more hours aboard the plane now depressed him. By this time in the flight all the food had started to look and taste the same and he only ate it to pass the time; nothing appeared to taste 'real' and everything had an unaccustomed false sweetness to it.

Jane was travelling a lot better than Hugo; she was sound asleep again and she passed the next few hours in sweet oblivion. By the time the flight had landed near the coast Hugo was thoroughly fed up with the plane's interior. He felt some ease when it was announced transit passengers would not be disembarking and they would only be waiting on the tarmac whilst other passengers were transferred and the plane was cleaned and re-fuelled.

"The next bit's only short Hugo, soon be there now," Rotherby-Hyde seemed annoyingly fresh and relaxed, as if he had just arrived downstairs for breakfast in his own home. Hugo's eyes felt sore and dry and despite having slept earlier he felt he had been awake for days on end. The captain then announced that their departure was delayed due to thick fog in Quito; Hugo's heart sank further. It was two hours later that they finally departed and flew the last short leg to Mariscal Sucre airport high in the Andes and in the centre of the city's buildings. Despite his fatigue and general bad mood, Hugo appreciated the captain's skill on his smooth landing on such a relatively short runway approached over mountainous terrain. He could now see why the place spent most of its mornings under a blanket of thick mist.

They took a taxi from the airport to their hotel and were installed there by lunchtime. Hugo and Jane showered and changed, then unpacked the minimum of their possessions and clothing that they would require overnight. They knew that the following morning they would be leaving again, returning to the airport for the short flight to Coca, something that they tried not to contemplate; they had done enough travelling in the last 24 hours. The strange atmosphere with its reduced level of oxygen, coupled with their tiredness, made the whole process hard work.

They met up again with Rotherby-Hyde in the lobby of the hotel at 1pm and he took them on to lunch at a local fish restaurant, just down the street from the hotel. `Limited Liability` still appeared fresh and in no way affected by his journey. He was obviously in good appetite and consumed the fresh sea bass that he had ordered with great enjoyment, whilst outlining what he had planned for them for the afternoon. Hugo and Jane were not really hungry and made a token effort with a bowl of `ceviche`, a local speciality dish, mainly consisting of different types of fish and shellfish marinated in citrus juices.

The rest of the afternoon was taken up with a tour of what Rotherby-Hyde called the main highlights of Quito. He showed them a variety of sights; cathedrals, monuments and government buildings with brightly dressed guards in old uniform were all on the agenda. All around the city seemed to spread on for ever, reaching into every hanging and valley of the mountains as far as the eye could see. The whole place was a continuous buzz of activity; the streets and roads were a constant stream of large four wheel drives, cars, buses and trucks and other vehicles, mainly of United States origin; but also from Europe and other parts of the world. There were even minivans in abundance, a sight Hugo had not seen since his youth. The almost 'too bright' stark sunlight that had beaten down on them for the first couple of hours, suddenly disappeared and dark rain clouds gathered quickly over the mountains around them. A few minutes later the rain was falling heavily.

"Where the hell did this lot come from? My skin was burning a few minutes ago."

"It always does that around three here, the weather's as changeable as England, only more predictable," Rotherby-Hyde laughed.

They were back at the hotel by 5.30pm; Hugo and Jane retired to their room, and after a token room service meal they went to bed, exhausted by the journey and the afternoon's activities. They did not intend to feel as tired again the following morning. Richard Rotherby-Hyde seemed to accept their decision to 'call it a day' with understanding good grace and bid them good night. The Lloyd's name was still awake several hours later, making phone calls and having long discussions.

# *Chapter Twenty One*

"AH Drew, how are you?" Richard Mowbray's familiar tone greeted Victor as he answered the telephone in the cottage.

"As it's that time of year when you've not much on, I've decided to make use of you over at the far woods; we've quite a bit of ground to make up due to the recent shortage of staff there and the season for selling logs will soon be over. We need to make the best of the time left." Victor accepted the news with some pleasure; he had been filling in time doing token tidying up around the shoot for the last few days, not really having any enthusiasm for starting the ground work in preparation for the following season. It all seemed a long way off and very uncertain too. He had come home early that afternoon, not feeling like spending the rest of the afternoon in the woods; even he had seen too much of them of late. The agent went on to say that the course of action had been agreed by Robbie Langdon and that it was likely that the keeper would now be employed more with general work around the estate than on the shoot for the time being, as `things were hanging in the balance` as he put it. This last announcement did not sit quite so well with Victor.

The following morning Victor drove over to the outlying woods on the edge of the estate beyond The Hall Wood and Home Farm. He reported to John Butcher who placed him with Simon Evans who was splitting logs and loading them onto a tipping trailer. The keeper felt awkward at first, not with the work, but with wondering how the woodsman was going to react to his presence. He had not really spoken to Simon at length since the incident with Roger and he wondered how he viewed it all and if he laid any blame at the keeper's door.

"Morning Simon, weather's looking good for this morning."

"Hi Vic, nice to have you with me; it's been too quiet here on my own since... you know?" Simon went quiet; he didn't need to explain further. Victor knew the big man was not as tough as his outward appearance seemed at that moment. The keeper nodded, pleased that his new workmate appeared to bear him no malice, but sad at seeing how things had affected him. Victor started to throw split logs onto the trailer, as Simon resumed feeding rounds of timber to the tractor mounted hydraulic splitter.

Midday saw the logging gang gathered at the edge of the clearing eating the simple contents of their lunch boxes and brewing hot strong tea. Driving back to the estate yard or anywhere else had been frowned upon by Mowbray as taking too much time out of the short winter days and they always ate in the woods, making full use of their short break. A group of four cock pheasants wandered out of the tree line at the far side of the clearing from the men. Victor watched them in silence as they scratched around for anything edible in the leaf litter. They always gave the impression to him that they knew the season was over and they had nothing much to fear from man at this time of year. He wondered if they would ever have anything to fear from a legally held gun ever again in Brockleston.

Victor left the woods in the late afternoon, aching in different places to normal and having at least had some company alongside him during his labours for a change. He stopped off at the 'Brockleston Arms' and consumed a well-earned pint of Old Steamer and a pork pie before heading home. His thirst slaked, there was little point in staying at the pub further; the place was empty apart from Bill Stewart who was busy sorting out the stock behind the bar and had only opened the place up as he was around to serve any passing trade. At that time of year 'The Brocky' was rarely open on weekday afternoons or early evenings.

# Chapter Twenty Two

UGO, JANE AND RICHARD ENTERED the arrivals' area at Coca airport, the intense humid heat of the rain forest basin already starting to make their light tropical shirts damp with perspiration. The short walk across the hot tarmac of the apron had been very different to that in the fresh warm breeze of the Caribbean night. Amongst the seemingly endless swathe of green-uniformed police officers bustling around officiously inside the building, a tall well-built native appeared and stepped forward, shaking Rotherby-Hyde's hand enthusiastically in greeting. This was Javier Manolito or `our man in Coca` as Jane's father had referred to him earlier. On seeing the greeting, the officers stepped back and ushered them through, one even carrying Jane's large canvas bag out onto the roadway for her. They were all travelling light, the bulk of their luggage having been left behind in storage at the hotel in Quito. Manolito led them to where a maroon Isuzu crew cab pickup stood and they placed their bags in the back before climbing in. Manolito drove them along the bustling road into the main town heading for the river. The traffic seemed to be as busy as it was in Quito, but now consisted of mainly older vehicles, many of which showed the signs of amateurish repairs and a `make do` attitude to maintenance out of pure necessity. There were dozens of small motorcycles and scooters, many of them ridden by young women, some dressed fashionably and with a lot of make-up adorning their naturally pretty faces. The roads in the town were lined with shops of all description, selling everything from food to car parts, their large hand-painted signs and brand promotions screaming their contents out in bright colours to passers by. The presence of oil had certainly made the town very active commercially and Hugo was put in mind of old images of the Klondike and similar places during the great gold rush that he had seen on history programmes. He got a complete feel for the place in that short drive; he felt the vibrancy of wealth generated by the black gold that was spreading down to even the poorest occupants of the town.

The vehicle stopped about a hundred yards from the river, by a large plain white rendered wall with a smart dark wood door that opened directly onto the street. The multi-coloured shops and intense activity had been left about half a mile behind and all that lay opposite was a large modern `office like` building; it was in the final stages of construction and its frontage consisted mainly of huge glass panels.

"They've built that with the hope of letting it out or selling it to one of the oil companies apparently; you never know it may be NapOil's one day soon Victor." Rotherby Hyde and Javier ushered them through the wooden door into a quiet courtyard. The tranquillity was striking, having just driven through the streets of the town. To the left hand side there was an open fronted covered area, with an expensive looking tiled floor. A number of chairs and tables stood in the cool shaded spot in front of a bar or counter area laid out with drinks and food. Opposite there was a toilet and shower block; a narrow garden with trellis and climbing plants decorated its outside wall.

"Please make yourself at home, we will rest for a while before taking our river trip, the boat is not here yet." Their local host spoke excellent English. He had the dark red skin and high cheek bones distinctive of many of the people from the area, giving his face an almost square appearance. His dark skin made his teeth appear bright white and this, coupled with his broad easy smile, made him amiable company. As they took their refreshment, Hugo engaged Javier in a conversation over the wildlife and geography of the area, which naturally then went onto the effect oil production was having on it. It turned out that Javier's main occupation was as a guide for one of the tourist lodges further up river and as such he could see both sides of the debate. His people were poor and although they were now starting to realise the value of their natural history, they were still in dire need of the employment and money that the oil industry had brought to the area. This conversation had obviously started to go too deep for Richard Rotherby-Hyde's liking.

"Alright Javier, that boat must have got here by now; shall we wrap things up here and get on our way!" They made their way out of the courtyard and walked the short distance to the edge of the

River. There was a tall embankment rising about 30 feet above the water. A well-made flight of old stone steps led down to the jetty below, turning twice at right angles as it did so. A strange selection of craft lay along the river's edge. There were long narrow motorised canoes with raised canopies consisting of a frame of metal rods topped with synthetic tarpaulins and strange raft-like vessels, one of which had the brightly painted fuselage of a small passenger jet secured onto it, presumably allowing any passengers to have the illusion of a low level flight along the river. This contraption gave the impression that it had not recently moved, if ever. There were also other more businesslike looking craft; small modern looking, high powered boats which were used as water taxis and serviced the workforce involved in oil abstraction and its associated activities. It was on one of these boats that they were to travel up river. Javier waved them off, having helped them aboard, and they sped off, rounding a bend in the river and heading away from sight of the town. The churning light brown water seemed to flow in a high speed torrent past the boat as it headed upstream; there were fallen trees hanging in the current that first appeared like strange creatures swimming against it. At intervals huge sandbanks arose from the water and the boat made huge zigzags across the vast width of the river avoiding these hazards and at times almost seeming to be going back on itself. Either side of the water lay jungle; tall trees, palms and other dense vegetation ran right down to the edge of the river, only occasionally interrupted by a small clearing or little cove with a nearby rustic dwelling standing out on the bank above it. There was the occasional motorised canoe, churning up the muddy water with its powerful outboard engine, showering its occupants with fine spray as it made its turns across the surface, taking visitors to and from the tourist lodges higher up the mighty waterway and also acting as free transport to the locals. What looked like a native mother and her two teenage daughters waved back at them as they passed.

After about an hour's travelling they started to come across maintenance platforms and other structures, either travelling or moored against the banks.

"Blimey, I've never seen the likes of that before, looks like madness!" Hugo pointed at the strange sight that was headed past them down river. Two huge articulated trucks were being carried on a sort of motorised barge, their wheels only inches from the water.

"Oh yes, common method of moving them about here; in fact the only one really; there are no roads through this part of the rain forest, hence our long river trip, everything gets moved via water." Victor nodded back at Rotherby-Hyde. He was enjoying this part of the trip; it wasn't like anything he had experienced before.

The boat slowed and headed towards the left hand bank, where a collection of steel framed buildings, site huts and vehicles stood near a large concrete jetty. They came alongside a row of lorry tyres hanging on ropes and the boat briefly moored up, allowing the three travellers and their baggage to leave it before it sped off again, heading further up river. As they walked towards the buildings a vehicle pulled onto the site and came to rest in front of them.

"Patrick, bang on time, well done." Rotherby-Hyde introduced the driver as Patrick Stephens, the development manager of Nap Oil. Stephens was an American who said that he had worked for one of the main oil companies in Texas and had now decided to do some prospecting for himself the other side of the Panama Canal, as he put it. Stephens drove them off down a muddy half made track away from the site, explaining the proposed layout and setting up of the planned oil abstraction as they went. So far the venture was looking pretty sound thought Hugo, despite the twinges he had over the destruction of parts of the forest; the journey up had appealed to his love of nature and wild places; the industrial installations he had seen stood out against the background of the forest like unsightly imposing invaders.

"There's not too much to see really, but I hope you can get an idea of the scale and potential of the proposed operation." Stephens and Rotherby-Hyde were in full flow with their `hard sell` as the Chevrolet four wheel drive bumped its way along the jungle road.

"This area is full of good sized oil deposits and we've been lucky to get in quickly enough to purchase this sector; all we need now is the government's permission to start abstracting so we can get on with the process of setting up the infrastructure to do it; we've almost got it, but a few dollars in the right direction might just speed things up." Stephens took them on a tour of a neighbouring oil operation and then to the edge of what looked like a totally undeveloped area of rain forest.

"The first thing we need to do is get a better road made to link us up properly with where you landed; all the equipment and supplies are ready to be shipped, but we need the go ahead first, no point in jumping the gun." Hugo and Jane were melting in the heat by this time; the late afternoon sun was beating down on the canopy and the humidity was very high from a heavy downpour the day before.

"I can see you've had enough for today; we'll head to my lodge and you can freshen up and we'll have some cold beers."

"Best offer I've had all day." Hugo smiled at the thought of getting out of his sweat drenched clothes and relaxing somewhere cooler.

After heading back the way they had travelled out, they turned onto a narrow track leading off the main half-made road and climbed up an incline. A short time later they arrived at a good sized wooden lodge with a roof composed of galvanised corrugated steel sheets. It looked pretty basic from the outside; but as they entered they could see that its austere appearance hid a fairly luxurious interior by local standards. The air inside was cooled and the furnishings comfortable.

"It's not a bad set-up now, just very noisy when it rains because of the roof; and unfortunately it does rain here with a vengeance as you would expect." The lodge was on one of the upper banks of the river and had an imposing view of the Napo; it was an impressive sight across the huge waterway as the sun started to set and the forest started to reverberate with the sounds of insects, frogs and other creatures. The ghostly calls of a nearby group of howler monkeys could be heard from the tree tops some distance away across the jungle.

"So how many companies are operating in the area Patrick?" Hugo had decided to start asking his own questions as they sat having dinner on the veranda at the front of the lodge.

"At least half a dozen I would say; hard to say exactly as some of them keep things pretty quiet like us, at least until they get going that is."

"Where are they from?"

"Mainly Ecuador, South America at least but the U.S has far

reaching interests as you know." Hugo continued his enquiries; Rotherby-Hyde kept quiet, sensing that his prospective son-in-law was now paying proper interest to the venture and it would not be long before they were talking hard currency.

They spent the night at the lodge, none of the English visitors getting much sleep, the noise of the jungle creatures and the demise of the air conditioning in the early hours doing nothing to contribute to a restful night. They were out early the following morning and caught the same boat from the little jetty now on its return trip back to Coca. After an uneventful flight back to the capital they spent the afternoon at the hotel, Hugo going through the facts and figures of the proposed investment with Richard, who had produced a large file from his room, showing what appeared to be detailed costings and projected income.

"Of course a lot depends on how much we can produce and the fluctuation in the world oil price, but I like to think we have looked on the conservative side of it all with these figures and it's fairly safe to say that the situation may be much better." Hugo had to admit that the figures made encouraging reading.

"Well as always, I would like a bit more time for it all to sink in, but I will admit I am now very interested. Can I borrow this and I will let you know in a few days?"

"By all means Hugo, but please let me know either way by the start of next week; as you saw for yourself there's  a lot riding on this."

The following day the three parted company; Hugo and Jane left for the airport in the mid-morning to catch a flight back to the Bahamas via Miami, leaving Rotherby-Hyde at the hotel. He said he had some loose ends to clear up and would be staying in Ecuador for a few days longer.

# Chapter Twenty Three

THE EVENTS OF THE RECENT months seemed very distant as Hugo and Jane sat relaxing in the saloon of the 'Lucy B', taking a cool drink after a mid afternoon swim. The greyness of England's late winter climate seemed almost unreal again, now that they were back in the Bahamas. To Hugo it felt like coming home, despite recently revisiting his ancestral roots. Being far removed from Brockleston both in time and distance allowed him to consider his situation more objectively, as objective as he could be when enjoying the luxury of relaxed living aboard his own boat once again that was.

"What do you think of it all Jane?"

"Think of what?"

"The Nap Oil thing; I doubt if Brockleston can service this lifestyle here for much longer; I need to get something in place for the future, but I'm not sure if I want to gamble the spare money that might support us for a while if things get too bad." Jane was no financial expert. However, her father up to the time she met Hugo had looked after her very comfortably and she knew that Richard was usually several steps ahead of the field when it came to innovative investment and speculation. His rise to enhanced prosperity following the Lloyds' crash was testament enough to this. She had no hesitation in commending the plan to Hugo; her father had never let her down. This was the final act in Hugo's decision-making process; his mind was made up.

Hugo got up and walked to the bar where his mobile phone lay ringing on the polished wood; no doubt it was Rotherby-Hyde calling to talk business, a conversation he was now ready for.

"Hello Hugo, heard you were back in the land of the sane, how's it all going?" It was Johnnie Marchington.

"Hi Johnnie, it's not looking too bad now at this end, been a pretty disturbing couple of months though I can tell you; where are you at the moment?"

"Anchored up in Exuma Sound just off Cat Island; you know I like it there."

"Stay there Johnnie, we'll get across to you in a couple of days, tell you all about things." Hugo rang off; he was going to try to get hold of Richard Rotherby-Hyde in Ecuador now that his mind was made up.

"Well, we think a sweetener of around $6,000,000 or so should get the minister's attention and let us get on with the job in hand."

"That's around £3,000,000; I think I can realise about £850,000 but no more, not without selling stuff off and that would take time even if I wanted to do that." Hugo suddenly felt very hot and uncomfortable now that they were talking in real figures; his free assets seemed insignificant now that he had entered the big arena usually frequented by Rotherby-Hyde and Melton.

"Don't worry too much Hugo, Jack and I can sort out the deficit if you can't make a full third up; all I really need to know is that you're in and can get the finances to me pretty quickly."

"Ok, I will get my accountants to contact you and they will arrange the transfer of the funds, if I deliberate any more I will never sort it out."

Rotherby-Hyde rang Jack Melton and added to the pleasure of his day; Jack's Comet had already romped home as a winner by four lengths at Haydock that afternoon.

Lord Brockleston's financial advisers were not happy at being left out of Hugo's decision. They would have liked to be consulted on using the bulk of his cash assets in a speculative foreign venture. They only tactfully referred to this in a passing conversation with Hugo over the logistics of transferring the funds to one of Jack Melton's company accounts. Like Jane, they had come to respect the astute dealings of Rotherby-Hyde over the years, having seen his successes.

By the beginning of March, Hugo was solely reliant on the income from the estate and just a few company shares he held elsewhere. The comfortable financial cushion that he had been resting on for many years had now been transferred into the hands of others and he did not feel good about the situation despite the constant reassurance of Jane. He did not share these concerns with his recently acquired business partners, who still seemed ebullient over the whole matter.

# *Chapter Twenty Four*

NICK JONES SAT IN THE back office of the front desk and reception area at Limcester Central Police Station. He had been forced to return to work on what they called 'light duties'. He knew the main purpose of this was to keep the division's sickness figures looking good and hence protect the Chief Superintendent's performance figures from being criticised by the `bean counters` at Headquarters. He had asked to do investigative work in the traffic office helping out his colleagues and being part of things again. Unfortunately for him someone had decided to monitor waiting times at the front desk and so in another effort to keep the managers happy his assignment was a foregone conclusion. For the past two weeks he had been taking reports of minor crimes, accidents, lost dogs and the interminable squabbling between neighbours. It brought back memories of when he was a probationer and the desk was permanently manned by police officers; he hadn't enjoyed doing it then and he certainly wasn't enjoying it now. As he completed a routine statement over the production of some driving documents, the bell rang again as it did with relentless regularity during the afternoon. He put down his pen and went to the desk. There was something strangely familiar about the woman that stood looking at him. She was attractive in a rough sort of way, but her face showed the distinctive signs of previous fist activity, the old distortions and scars detracting from her looks in good light.

"Hello Nick, didn't expect to see you here like this." It was Sarah Stokes. She wanted to see DCI Bob Lewis.

"I saw a piece in the paper the other day. I can't believe what's happened on the shoot, I didn't think they would go that far. How's Vic doing?" Nick Jones took Sarah to a side interview room and then brought her a cup of coffee.

"I will go and see if I can find Mr Lewis for you, won't be

long I hope." It was 15 minutes before PC Jones managed to find the DCI.

"I've got a Sarah Stokes down at the front desk Sir, she would like to speak to you."

"What's that old tart want? Tell her I'm not here."

"She says she's seen the appeal in the paper for information on the Brockleston job." Lewis got to his feet and hurried down the four flights of stairs.

"Thanks Jones."

This was what Bob Lewis needed to know; only one witness and mostly circumstantial evidence, but plenty to create a chink in the erstwhile high security of Hampton's no comment account of the affair. He treated Sarah like royalty, bringing her more coffee and writing down her statement himself. The first statement he had taken himself for nearly ten years.

An hour later Hampton looked up from his pint of cider at the figure of DCI Bob Lewis standing in between two traffic officers in the bar of 'The Unicorn' pub on the Brandley Park Estate. Before he could come out with one of his usual well used insults the senior detective spoke.

"Scott Hampton, I am arresting you on suspicion of the manslaughter of Roger McAlister." He then administered the usual caution. Hampton was silent as the two uniformed officers stood him up, handcuffed him and marched him out to the waiting patrol car. It was the first time he had been arrested without at least some token struggle occurring.

# Chapter Twenty Five

ROBBIE LANGDON SPENT THE FIRST few months of the year trying to keep the shoot members together and to gather enough funding to secure its future. He knew that unless he could satisfy Mowbray that the next season at Brockleston would be going ahead as usual, he would not be able to get Victor returned to his game keeping duties soon enough to have all the pens, feeders and infrastructure ready for the new birds to arrive in May. The agent had moved Victor on from the logging gang in early spring and onto general estate maintenance duties, often working alongside Arthur Young and John Wrench on the estate properties. Five members of the shoot had already resigned their membership and three more were considering it. Word had spread of the winter's events at Brockleston and advertisements in the shooting press had not generated any interest; so there were no prospective new members.

The interest in the shoot that Hugo had developed around Christmas and New Year had now been replaced by his concern over the large new investment; and Mowbray once again had a free hand to manage the running of the estate as he thought best. By the beginning of June it was clear that there would not be a shooting season that year at Brockleston. Victor would often walk the woods in an evening out of habit, stepping over the briars that were spreading across the rides and longing to be checking the new poults in the release pens. But there were no young pheasants in the woods apart from the few that had been bred in the wild, somehow managing to avoid the attentions of the foxes and other predators that now had free rein over the shoot.

Mowbray had already started to make tentative enquiries into other uses that could be made of the woods and the shoot's modest facilities. He wanted to have something substantial and financially sound to put to his lordship before committing himself to any course of action; so at least this was progressing slowly. As it was the agent's efforts were to seem like tiny ripples on a pond compared to the huge rip tide that was about to sweep across the estate.

"Victor, bad news I'm afraid old boy, it's all gone belly up!" Hugo gripped the phone handset so tightly that his knuckles were showing white and the plastic casing was only just holding out from shattering. Richard Rotherby-Hyde spoke with an annoyingly easy manner, imparting the bleak news to his daughter's life partner as if he was merely refusing a stranger's insurance proposition. Hugo sat down on the sun lounger, his face managing to become ashen despite his tan.

"What the hell am I going to do now? That was all I had, what the hell's gone wrong?" Lord Brockleston's composure went completely; anger and despair overtook him. Rotherby-Hyde then went on to list a catalogue of problems they had come across. These culminated with the Ecuadorian Government listening to ecological arguments from pressure groups; and the expansion of oil abstraction in that area being put on hold indefinitely. Rotherby-Hyde than rang off, tactfully allowing Hugo to come to terms with the loss of his funds, considering it too early to launch the final phase of his and Jack Melton's plan to get hold of part of the Brockleston Estate for development. The offer to buy part of it as a favour due to the failed investment being partly their fault was to come later that week, after Hugo had time to worry about his future for a few days.

# Chapter Twenty Six

THE TRUE VALUE OF A man is measured not by his wealth in either material or intellectual property, but by the regard he has for other living creatures around him; whether they are from his own species or another, no matter how insignificant they may seem. A reverence for the traditions and values of past generations which they have built up over the centuries is essential to the very fabric of our being if we are to survive and prosper, not only as individuals but also as a society. Sound, fair and responsible interaction has always been the only productive route forward. But there have always been and always will be those that would squander the inheritance of all for their own selfish ends, their fleeting existence on the planet leaving an indelible stain for all to see, except those whose own desires render them blind. Countless lives pass with each generation, most unnoticed by the millennia. A few are remembered and celebrated for their contribution to the greater good, their names and works passed down through the ages. The deeds of some whose names are rarely mentioned reach down the years to impoverish our lives still. The long forgotten sleepers in Graves Spinney left no lasting mark on Brockleston during their fleeting time in its secluded acres. The previous generations at the Hall did at least ensure some had a good living, albeit a hard one at times, and their years gave structure and social history to all around them. The dark, cold hand of avarice that had reached out to hold the estate in its calculating grasp would now leave its hateful mark, obliterating all that had gone before.

The huge iron wrecking ball swung through the back wall of the shoot shed, the old whitewash shattering in a cloud of choking dust as the bricks burst, taking with it all record of the old names and dates scrawled on its cobwebbed surface. Home Farm's time had come, the bulldozers and demolition plant making short work of the old farm and estate yard buildings. They were not suitable for conversion to luxury barn dwellings and so would play no part in the grand scheme of Brockleston's development, apart from providing land for a new leisure complex and golf driving range that were planned for the site, the previous years of sporting activities swept away to make room for new, more socially acceptable pursuits in these enlightened times. Victor stood at the roadside, a lone figure watching in silent mourning the final passing of his former life as gamekeeper. This was it, the final act in the play that had unfolded over the last twelve months, he thought to himself as he peered through the temporary safety fencing. Great plumes of grey smoke billowed from pyres where ancient oak beams burned amongst old window frames and doors, torn from their dark homes in the roof spaces of the buildings, seeing the sunlight again briefly before they were rendered to grey ash. Crushing machines reduced the bricks and rubble to hardcore as they fed greedily on the estate's architectural history. Victor cursed himself for coming to see the spectacle, but knew he had to witness it. It was like paying his last respects to something he had lived with all his life, grown up with, grown into, and then not had the chance to grow out of, even if he had wanted to. He had walked down to Home Farm; it helped to pass the time. There was now very little to fill his days apart from trawling through sporting magazines and any other source of advertisements for suitable employment. He was not yet ready to admit it to himself but his prospects of finding employment in his chosen profession were bleak; soon he would have to start looking at anything that he might be capable of doing to earn money. He was not old enough yet to sit back and enjoy a retirement, with an additional bit of income from a side line of pest control like old Bill Flemming had been. He was finding it difficult to meet the rent on the cottage that was now being asked for by the estate's new owners. Gone were the days of a tied cottage without a charge since his employment ended and his meagre redundancy payment was rapidly being spent on just existing.

As he turned to walk back to the village he said his last goodbye to the old farm and strode without purpose back towards home. He doubted if he would be able to face seeing the place again and regretted that he had not left it standing in his memory; witnessing its destruction was perhaps not something he should have subjected himself to but he had done it now and there was no going back.

Victor got back into the village at just after 1pm. Instead of heading for Keeper's Cottage he turned left and went into the 'Brockleston Arms'. The pub was busy as it had been on most weekday lunchtimes since the start of the new developments at Brockleston. There were nearly always demolition or construction workers in the bar and often surveyors, architects and the like having an expense account lunch in the lounge. It wasn't now really the sort of place Victor enjoyed being in, but it was better than going straight back to the solitude of home. At least one part of the old Brockleston was thriving, although with a much changed clientele, he thought to himself. Bill Stewart was serving at the bar and appeared under pressure with the sheer volume of customers. It had been several weeks since his trade had increased out of all proportion, but he still did not appear to have become accustomed to the level of activity. The landlord had been trying to recruit new staff to cope with the increased trade but with limited success. He had even offered Victor a job one evening when he was in the bar. The former keeper had laughed at the time; but he was starting to think about it a lot more seriously now; he could perhaps out of necessity now tolerate Bill's references to ill winds and clouds with silver linings. The licensee had not been able to hide his pleasure in the increased profits despite knowing that many other local people were now without work and most were having to move away to find what employment they could.

Victor took his pint of Old Steamer and sat by the fire. At least there was still something of the old place left. He quickly flicked through the local weekly paper that he had picked up from the bar. There was very little in it for him in terms of jobs; he hadn't yet fallen to the level of contract chicken catching at huge factory-like poultry rearing farms although it was about all he was qualified to do of the positions advertised there. He sat staring into the flames, oblivious to the loud hum of raucous conversation around him. By the third pint he was starting to feel the effects of the alcohol. He hadn't eaten that day and the strong dark ale caressed him into the sense of detached well-being that so many had fallen in love with to their cost. He drank on into the afternoon; the pub was now quiet again, and the workers were back at their labours of transformation. Time continued at its ancient constant pace as the late November day darkened to its usual conclusion.

"Come on Vic, you've had enough lad, time you got yourself home," the landlord's voice sounded distant; it was some seconds before Victor realised where he was again; he had fallen asleep in the warmth and the beer.

"It's nearly half three, we're closing up, can't keep the place open just for you." Victor got to his feet and stumbled out of the bar. It was still light enough to see and the lights inside the pub had been dim so he had no difficulty making out the features of the lane that led to home. The cold air struck him and he felt the full effects of what he had consumed; his legs struggled to propel him homeward as he staggered out of the village centre towards the cottage. He had not felt that drunk since the night he and Nick Jones had gone out on a patrol of the woods after drinking heavily on a shoot day; the night they had found old Storm's body in the woods.

He staggered on in his drunken state, his mind and emotions working overtime, his legs struggling to keep up. When he got to the small close of houses where Sarah Stokes had once lived he stopped and stood looking at her old home.

"Something else that was just taken from me," he said to himself before staggering on. He stumbled towards the centre of the lane; there was a sound of screeching tyres and a car horn sounded.

"Watch out, you bloody idiot." The words drifted back to him on the wind from a car window opened to hurl the abuse. It was almost dark when he got to Keeper's Cottage. The walk had done nothing to decrease the effects of the alcohol and if anything he was more under its influence now. He fell through the door and snatched up a bottle of whisky that was on the kitchen table.

"Let's have a drink together to mark the end of the last season old lad." He strode purposefully out of the door, through the unkempt garden and struggled over the fence into the fields behind the cottage. An old familiar feeling of peace and contentment greeted him; he was again in his world, alone with his thoughts in the night, on familiar paths across the fields and through the woods. He stuffed the whisky bottle into the pocket of his coat.

"Not a drop until I get there, I won't drink alone." Walking on past Graves Spinney and the back of St John's church he passed through the early dark of the night. A pair of eyes reflecting the moonlight crossed the field just up ahead, stopping briefly to stare at him before moving on quickly, having realised it was a man. A man with a familiar smell, a man who had hunted him on many nights in the past, an old adversary he hadn't seen for many months now.

"It's all yours now, Charlie, my old mate. I won't be bothering you again; keep it well, enjoy it while it lasts and God bless your cubs."

Victor reached Lady Jane's Moss and crossed into the blackness of the tree cover. There was the familiar sound of a startled pheasant as he entered the wood. It would be some years before there were little or no game birds left at Brockleston despite the days of them being released now being over. The pheasant was a wily old bird, especially for a species that wasn't native to Britain. There were always some that managed to avoid both two and four legged predators to breed in the wild. He walked on through the wood, travelling as skilfully as he ever had done, making his way to the ride. He stepped out from the trees onto the narrow strip that had been the scene of countless good pheasant drives; it was overgrown and uncared for. The briars had enjoyed a good summer and there had been no cutting back done to clear the path prior to the new season, as there wasn't going to be one that year. The solitary figure of the keeper negotiated the spiked stems that constantly caught across his ankles, slowing his progress. There was now no need to hide in the tree line, no need for concealment; that little game had now reached its conclusion, with him on the losing side. He came to a too familiar stretch of the path and stared into the gloom searching for a marked place. His eyes soon found what he sought. A short hand-made stake stood out of the peaty ground just to the side of the ride; on it there was a worn dog collar hanging from a rusty nail which had been bent upwards to form a hook after being driven into the wood. He reached down and touched the collar, letting the old waxy leather slide between his fingers. "Here we are, old lad, bet you thought I had forgotten you; no chance of that." Victor went to the nearest tree and sat down, facing the grave with his back resting against the wide trunk. He took out the bottle and removed the top, throwing it into the bushes before taking a long hard pull of the spirit.

"Here's to us and days gone by Storm; it was good while it lasted. I suppose we were lucky; there are those that will never see the like of it." The keeper drank on in silence; soon the bottle was empty and he slumped to the ground at the base of the tree. The darkness overtook him as the spirit surged through his brain. He lapsed into unconsciousness on the cold, damp peaty earth.

Victor was positioning the guns at The Moss on a crisp end of January morning, Storm was following at his heels and all the old faces were there for the beaters' day. The dream faded, lapsing into a dark, unfeeling, unthinking nothing He could feel himself smiling as all sensation and thought passed away.

Close by a tiny mammal was crossing the Brockleston Road. As the creature neared the safety of the hedgerow its life was cut short by the tyre of a passing car. The vehicle travelled on through the darkness towards Limcester, its driver as oblivious of this unintentional act of slaughter as the shrew had just become of its former tenuous existence in the world.

*Nicholas Gordon*
*4<sup>th</sup> March 2008*

# MELROSE BOOKS

## If you enjoyed this book you may also like:

### The Militiaman
Alexander Bayly

*The Militiaman* is about Robert Edwards, a recently retired government scientist whose whole world is turned upside down by a devastating family tragedy. As he struggles to come to terms with his loss, the miscreant responsible for Robert's misfortune is himself killed. This has all the hallmarks of summary justice and Robert is inevitably treated as a suspect. In the meantime, to help him to rebuild his life Robert makes a return to his previous employment with the Ministry of Defence, involving occasional nocturnal pursuits to assist M16 in their dealings with the shady underworld of the illicit arms trade. Numerous other reprisals and executions occur over a period of two years or so, which follow social injustices closely related to Robert during his rehabilitation and which increasingly point to him being responsible for the retributions.

Size: 234 mm x 156 mm        Pages: 96
Binding: Royal Octavo Hardback      ISBN: 978-1-906050-75-7      £12.99

### The Abbot
Tony Rycroft

Following the 9/11 terrorist attacks in New York, the British government commissioned research into developing anti-viruses for anthrax, fearing a terrorist attack on the UK mainland involving a biological weapon.

When the chief scientist working on experiments steals the most deadly virus ever created, he sparks a massive operation involving the police, the military and a tiny village in Cambridgeshire.
But when it is stolen a second time and no one knows who was responsible, things turn from bad to impossible.

Size: 234 mm x 156 mm        Pages: 224
Binding: Royal Octavo Hardback      ISBN: 978-1-905226-10-8      £8.99

### Four Aces: Life in the East End
Roy S. Purcell

*Four Aces* is about four young men living in the East End of London. Having grown up together and despite being employed and having girlfriends, they still spend a great deal of time as a group
Due to the small wages they earn, the boys become involved in petty crimes to supplement their income, developing a taste for luxury items. They begin to enjoy life while they are still young.

However, decisions are made that affect their friendship, dramatically changing their lives.

Size: 234 mm x 156 mm        Pages: 224
Binding: Royal Octavo Hardback      ISBN: 978-1-906561-15-4      £14.99

**St Thomas' Place, Ely, Cambridgeshire CB7 4GG, UK**
**www.melrosebooks.com   sales@melrosebooks.com**